# THE MISTLETOE MOTIVE

*A Holiday Novella*

## CHLOE LIESE

# CONTENTS

# AUTHOR'S NOTE

**\*Includes spoilers\***

This holiday romance is open door, meaning it portrays on-page, consensual sexual intimacy. It also features characters with human realities that I believe deserve to be seen more prominently in romance through positive, authentic representation—in this case, neurodivergence (specifically, autism, which is my lived experience), the asexual spectrum (specifically, demisexuality, which is also my lived experience), and type 1 diabetes (which has been informed by a friend with this condition). With the guidance of my own experience and authenticity readers for this content, I hope I have given these subjects the care and respect they deserve.

This book also includes mention of an ex who texts repeatedly after being broken up with and who, in one scene, shows up unannounced, surprising the heroine. He is reprimanded, and after that, is off-page, out of her life for good. I know this is a sensitive topic for some, so please take care.

Ultimately, I hope this romance brings you comfort and

joy, a story of two people finding their way toward being deeply known and loved for all of who they are, which is, to me—in real life and in fiction—the greatest gift we can receive.

# PLAYLIST NOTE

At the beginning of each chapter, a song and artist is provided as an optional means of emotional connection to the story. It isn't a necessity—for some it may be a distraction or even inaccessible—nor are the lyrics literally about the chapter. Listen before or while you read for a soundtrack experience. If you enjoy playlists, rather than searching for each song individually as you read, you can directly access these songs on a Spotify Playlist by logging in to your Spotify account and entering "The Mistletoe Motive" into the search browser.

# CHAPTER 1

## PLAYLIST: "LET IT SNOW! LET IT SNOW! LET IT SNOW!" ELLA FITZGERALD

The world is a snow globe. Thick, icy flakes swirl around me, drifting from a silver tinsel sky. A frigid gust of wind stings my cheeks and whips my clothes. It's my morning walk to Bailey's Bookshop, where I am co-manager and resident holiday enthusiast, and I'm kicking off the month of December like I have for years: my mittened hands wrapped around a cup of peppermint hot cocoa—chocolate drizzle, extra whip—while Ella Fitzgerald's smoky-sweet voice pours through my headphones.

*Let it snow! Let it snow! Let it snow!*

Wrangling open the door to the bookshop as the song ends and Ella's voice fades, I tug off my noise-cancelling headphones, whose plush, winter-white faux fur makes them double as earmuffs. Time to face reality: this wonderful life of holiday tunes, picturesque snowfall, and running Bailey's Bookshop would be a dream come true, if it weren't for one small thing...

My gaze lands on the familiar terrain of towering height, broad shoulders, and starched, snowy cotton.

Okay. So he's not exactly *small*.

"Miss Di Natale." The chill of my antagonist's voice slips down my spine like a waterdrop, fresh off an icicle.

I shut the door with my butt, then use my elbow to slide down the bolt and lock us in, since we don't open for another hour. Clutching my hot cocoa and a canvas bag of homemade holiday decorations for festive fortitude, I reply with false cheer, "Mr. Frost."

My aptly named nemesis glances meaningfully at the antique wall-mounted clock, which sets his face in profile. Strong nose, cheekbones that could shave ice, a cut-crystal jaw. One dark eyebrow arches as he turns and his wintergreen eyes pin me in place. "Good of you to join us...three minutes late."

I hate him. He is the prickly holly leaf in the Fraser fir garland of my life.

For twelve torturous months, I have endured co-managing the city's longest-standing independent bookstore with Jonathan Frost, a true Scrooge of a man, and frankly I'd call it a miracle that I've lasted this long without going off the deep end.

Holding his eyes, I take a long, wet slurp of my hot cocoa's whipped cream, then lick my lips, because it'll get under his skin, and after that "three minutes late" reprimand, it's the least he deserves.

His gaze snaps to my mouth. His jaw twitches. Then he spins away.

"Let me guess." His voice is gruff, his eyes on an unopened box of new releases as he flicks up the retractable blade of a utility knife and guts the box like a fish belly, with one clean rip down the seam. "They messed up your overpriced choco-late milk."

My molars grind as I march across the storefront. "It's *hot cocoa*. And they forgot the peppermint. I can't kick off the holiday season without it."

After I've passed him, he guts the next box with the fluid grace of a cold-blooded killer. I watch him slide down the retractable blade, set the knife perpendicular to the edge of the counter, then wrench open the box in a graphic display of flexing muscles beneath his shirt.

It's a tragedy that such a lump-of-coal personality has a body like that.

"Eyes up, Gabriella."

"I'm watching that utility knife."

"Sure you are."

My cheeks heat. I set the holiday decorations on the counter with the force of my annoyance and hear one crack. "Anyone who knew how many slashers you read, Mr. Frost, would have their eyes on the utility knife."

"So she's not only eyeing up my muscles but my private bookstore purchases."

"I—" An infuriated growl rolls out of me. But as I spin away from him and freeze, my fury melts when I notice a plate of delicate sugar cookies perched on the counter. Cut into shapes that are an homage to every wintertime holiday, they sparkle with diamond-bright sugar crystals. Bending for a closer look, I breathe them in. Rich, buttery, sweet. I can already taste them melting on my tongue. "Where did these come from?"

"One guess." Jonathan hoists both boxes up on his shoulders, making more distracting muscly things happen under his shirt.

I turn back to face the mystery cookies, lest I get accused of ogling his ass while he walks to the shelves dedicated to new releases. Wracking my brain, I set down my hot cocoa, then shuck off my mittens, scarf, and coat, and hang them on their usual hook. I pluck one of the cookies from the plate, inspecting it. "The Baileys?"

Jonathan sighs wearily.

"What? That's a perfectly reasonable guess!"

The bookshop's owners, Mr. and Mrs. Bailey, don't come in often, but they're thoughtful and like grandparents to me. I've worked for them for six years, first part-time while in college, then the past two years, since graduating, as manager. They know how much I love December, all things holiday, and of course, sweets. I could see them having cookies delivered to the store for us (they're fond of Jonathan, too, for some baffling reason).

So, if *they* didn't send the cookies, then who? There's no one else anymore, thanks to an extra-tight budget this year and the fact that our only help, a part-time college student, quit last week. Apparently, Clark found Jonathan's and my dynamic "toxically hostile."

Kids these days. No stomach for conflict.

"Well, then, Mr. Frost." I examine the cookie. "If not from the Baileys, where *did* they come from?"

Jonathan *tsks*, lining up a perfectly even row of books. "'One guess,' Gabriella, means 'one guess.'"

Perplexed but enticed by the heavenly sugar-cookie aroma, I almost take a bite. Then I pause. A lightbulb pings over my head. Pointing the cookie his way, I level Jonathan with a suspicious glare. "You."

He pauses, the book he's holding frozen in midair. Slowly, he glances over his shoulder, and our gazes snag. His face is...unreadable.

While people's expressions aren't easy for me to interpret, the longer I know them, the better I'm able to observe patterns and memorize their meaning. After twelve miserable months observing the many subtle shifts in his chiseled-from-ice features, I know more Jonathan Frost expressions than I care to admit. This one is new.

Unsettled, I bite my bottom lip, a lick of pain to ground myself. I watch his gaze lower to my mouth, his eyes darken.

All of a sudden, I'm roasting in my emerald-green sweater dress. Is the heat cranked up?

"If you *did* bring these cookies..." I'm trying to regain the upper hand, but my voice is oddly hoarse. "The question is...why?"

Jonathan's gaze flicks up and meets mine. Another expression I don't recognize. It makes my belly tumble.

He opens his mouth, like he's about to answer me, when a fist bangs on the shop's front door. Jonathan scowls in its direction and barks, "Closed till ten!"

The room's cooler now, and the clutch of whatever mind tricks Jonathan was playing with his eyes has vanished. Sensible and back in my skin, I drop the cookie like a hot potato, brush crumbs from my hands, and stride toward the front door.

"Too scared to try one?" he drawls.

He has to have brought them. He probably baked them from scratch just so he could stick a laxative in the batter.

"The day I eat something you made will be a cold day in hell, Mr. Frost. And just so you know, poisoning someone is a criminal offense."

He's back at the shelves, lining up books with tidy precision. "If it's nonfatal, you only serve a few years."

I trip into the door, yelling, "I knew it!"

"Honestly, Gabriella." He rolls his eyes. "I *read* thrillers. Doesn't mean I want to be in one."

"I'm still hiding the box cutters."

As I'm about to unlock the door, I catch my reflection in its pane of frosted glass. Between this morning's windswept walk to work and Jonathan's mind games, I look like I walked through a tornado: cheeks flushed as rosy as my lips; hazel eyes saucer-wide, blinking frantically; my hair's honey-brown, loose curls, which usually sit at my shoulders, look electrified.

"Yeesh." As I fuss with my hair and command my eyes to

look less deranged, a prickle of awareness dances up my neck. Jonathan's eyes lock with mine in the glass reflection. He throws me another chilly arched eyebrow. I stick out my tongue.

"Real mature," he says.

"Coming from the guy leaving some poor delivery person to freeze on the sidewalk."

Jonathan—shocker—is a hard-ass who won't answer the door until opening, but sometimes delivery people get turned around and can't find the alley entrance. I'm the sympathetic one who helps them out.

With a wrench of the bolt, I open the door to the sight of a delivery person—their legs at least—staggering under the weight of a bouquet that dwarfs their upper body.

A voice from behind it says, "Delivery for Miss Gabriella Di Natale?"

I stare at it, slack-jawed. This is hundreds of dollars in flowers. Crimson roses and velvet poinsettias, cheery sprigs of pine and holly, snow-white lilies the size of dinner plates. Their cloying scent hits my nose, and a vicious sneeze doubles me over.

A warm, house-sized torso reaches past me as another sneeze wracks my body. Jonathan grips the tapered vase like it's a twig rather than thirty pounds of floral opulence and goes straight for the note wedged inside. I'm equally curious to know who it's from—his guess is as good as mine.

"Um, but..." The delivery person finally peeks around the bouquet. "This is for Miss Gabriella Di..." Their voice dies off in the face of Jonathan's arctic glare. "I need a signature."

"Does she look like she can sign?" Jonathan jerks his head toward me as I double over in another sneeze, then signs with a flourish. "Gabriella, tell them I'm not stealing your flowers."

"He's not. It's fine. Thank—*ah-ah-ah-CHOO*."

"Happy holidays," Jonathan says, as he shuts the door in

their face. "Last time I show up December first with a baked-good olive branch. You accuse *me* of poisoning you with cookies, when your boyfriend's the one gifting you a biohazard." He crosses the store toward the back, systematically plucking each lily from the bouquet. "Some fella you've got yourself."

I double over in a sneeze that rattles my sinuses. "W-what?"

"Knows you well enough to send a holiday-themed bouquet but not well enough to make sure it's low fragrance. Strong scents make you sneeze and trigger your headaches."

"He's not—Wait. How do *you* know that?"

"Twelve months, Miss Di Natale." Jonathan sets the bouquet on the counter, whips open the back door to the alley, and flings a hundred dollars' worth of lilies into the dumpster like they're vermin.

"Twelve months *what*?" I ask.

After shutting the door, he strolls into the break room kitchenette where we keep a coffee pot and mugs, along with a cabinet of snacks whose shelves are divided down the middle by boundary-defining tape, like we're feuding countries and the corner of a Triscuit box encroaching on enemy territory is cause for war.

Jonathan flicks on the water at the sink and rolls up his sleeves to his elbows, each fold of crisp, white cotton revealing two new inches of corded muscles and a dusting of dark hair. I tell myself to stop staring, but I can't.

Besides my two best friends, who are also my roommates, the only person I spend this much time with is Jonathan Icicle-Up-His-Butt Frost, and I think it's warping my brain—day in and day out, eight eternal hours around him. Brushing elbows as we pass each other in the store. Watching him grunt and flex all those muscles as he opens boxes and stocks shelves. Catching his eyes narrowed at me when I break the rules and plop on the floor with a tiny customer, cracking open a book to read to them.

Sometimes in those unspoken moments, things like this happen. My mind wipes away fifty-two weeks of daily squabbles and petty power battles and takes an inexplicable turn, like fixating on his forearms, staring at his hands as they slip and rub under the water. And then I start to think about other times arms flex and hands get wet. I think about fingers curling, and now his thumb's circling a splotch of ink on his palm, and I'm thinking about his thumb circling *other* things and—

"Twelve months." His voice thunder-cracks through the air, and I straighten like lightning just zapped my spine. "Fifty-two weeks. Six days a week. Eight hours each day. Two thousand four hundred and ninety-six hours." Eyes on his task, he flicks off the water, frees a paper towel from the stand with a vicious rip, then dries his hands. "Believe it or not, I've picked up a few things along the way."

Steeling myself, I fold my arms across my chest. "I see. 'Keep your friends close, your enemies closer.' Isn't that the saying?"

Jonathan glances up and meets my eyes, his gaze speaking some cryptic language that I don't.

I *hate* that feeling. It's old and familiar, and it never fails to scrape open the scab of my social struggles. I'm a neurodivergent girl in a neurotypical world, and my autistic brain doesn't read people the way Jonathan Tactical-Mastermind Frost's does. It's one of the very first things that made me dislike him: I can *feel* his cunning, his cold, calculating mind. He has what I don't, he sees what I can't, and he wields those weapons ruthlessly. It's exactly why the Baileys hired him.

Because he's everything I'm not.

And in my worst moments, that makes me feel like *I'm* not enough.

I wanted to be everything the Baileys needed when Mrs. Bailey retired from managing and they promoted me. The Baileys wanted that, too. They love me. They love how I love the bookshop. And their bottom line would certainly be healthier with only one manager in this day and age that's swiftly killing independent bookstores.

But after my first year solo, seeing I was drowning in the deluge of managerial tasks, the Baileys sat me down over tea and said it was too much to ask of one person—I deserved a co-manager.

So Jonathan was hired, exactly one year ago today. Bursting with holiday excitement, I walked in, only to see him chumming it up with Mr. Bailey, a rosy pink in Mrs. Bailey's cheeks as he said something that made her smile. I'd been usurped. It hit me like a snowball to the solar plexus.

He's been here ever since, making the Baileys fall in love with him, proving himself indispensable. He's confident and coolly efficient, and after a year under his influence, Bailey's Bookshop runs like a well-oiled machine.

Jonathan's the brain of this place. I admit that.

But me? I'm the *soul*.

I'm the whimsical touches in the window display, the thoughtful addition of plush armchairs tucked into cozy corners. I'm the warm smile that welcomes you and the artful front display table that draws you in. And Jonathan knows it. He knows that without me, this place would be industrious but impersonal, tidy but tedious.

In short: he needs me just as badly as I need him.

I realize that sounds like a great reason to join forces and set aside differences. But since The Dreaded Chain Bookstore (also known as Potter's Pages) came into the neighborhood two years ago and our profits took a hit, I know it's only a matter of time until the Baileys break the news that they can no longer afford both of us. And like hell am I going to have surrendered my place, to have allowed Jonathan Frost to become the dominant force that makes the Baileys' choice between us a no-brainer.

Meaning, that while our feud might have started out as a clash of personalities, it's now a duel to the death.

Er. Professional death, that is.

A drip of water from the faucet falls with a *plink*, wrenching my mind from its meandering path.

I realize I've been staring at Jonathan.

And Jonathan's been staring back.

Apparently, we've been doing this for some time, judging by the way the world starts to blur and my eyes scream for me to blink.

Jonathan, of course, because he's made of some cryogenic alien substance, looks entirely at ease as he leans in the door-way, arms folded across his chest. He could do this all day. Blinking is for the weak.

Unable to ignore my eyeballs' plea for mercy, I spin toward the massive floral arrangement and blink rapidly, barely choking back a relieved whimper as I pivot the vase and inspect it. That's when I spot a small card wedged inside the blossoms. I've been so frazzled by Jonathan, I forgot to look for the note explaining who this is from.

My hand is halfway to the card when Jonathan says, "Wait."

Frozen in place, I sense him behind me. Not so close that it's inappropriate or invasive, but close enough to feel his solid warmth behind me, to breathe in his faint wintry-woods scent. I hate that so many smells give me headaches, but Jonathan's is undeniably pleasurable.

Reaching past me, he tugs the poinsettia away from the plastic clip holding the card. "Careful."

I glance up and meet his eyes. They're evergreen dark, his jaw tight. Under the shop's warm lights, I catch a glimmer of auburn in the bittersweet-chocolate waves of his hair. "Careful of what?" I ask.

"Poinsettia. They can cause a rash."

I snort. "A rash."

"A rash, Gabriella." He juts his chin toward the note. "I told you, I'm not the one you have to worry about. Your boyfriend sent your sinuses' worst nightmare and toxic plants."

There it is again. My *boyfriend*.

Trey and I haven't been together for six months, and even before that, "together" was a generous term. I'm someone who needs time to feel out my attraction, and while I was certainly struck by Trey, the smiling, golden-haired guy who bought my hot cocoa one morning at the coffee shop where I'd seen him ordering his latte, I wasn't sure how I felt about dating him. But Trey was persistent, and soon he was buying my drink every morning, texting me all day, sending a private car to wait outside the bookshop after work, ready to whisk me his way so he could wine and dine me.

Which, in retrospect, was a red flag. I'd communicated the need for time to figure out how I felt. Trey only pursued me more fervently. And for two months, I let the appealing routine of our dinners out and conversations, being texted and checked in on, dull the warning signals blaring in my brain. I reasoned with myself, we'd turned out okay, hadn't we? Sure, he'd pursued me a little aggressively, but most people I knew didn't need the time that I did.

Being demisexual, I experience attraction less frequently and differently than most others seem to. It takes me a while to know whether I find someone attractive or desire them sexually, if I like the scent of their skin or the feel of their hand touching mine or the idea of being physically intimate. Any time I've experienced that kind of desire, it's come after

I've bonded with that person, established connection and familiarity. And that takes time to sort out.

Trey simply didn't understand that, and I clearly hadn't done a good enough job explaining myself. Or so I thought, back then. Now I know better—that what I'd told him should have been enough, that a good partner would have honored my boundaries, not steamrolled right over them.

Jonathan picked up that I was seeing someone. Trey never came by the shop, which made me a little sad since Bailey's is my pride and joy, but he said he was busy and worked on the other side of town in finance, that the one morning he'd gotten a coffee from my local haunt was because of a meeting with clients, but now I made driving across town for coffee every morning entirely worth it.

I'd get flowers—and yes, they always made me sneeze—with sappy poem notes. He texted me and called enough for it to be obvious there was someone in my life.

But it wasn't until our summer sale, when I was running around busily, that Jonathan realized who it was when he saw Trey's name come up on my phone.

I'd watched him point at my cell, then pin me with that arctic glare. "Who's that?"

"Not that it's any of your business..." I'd snatched my phone off the counter. "But it's the guy I've been seeing."

"*That's* who you're with," he'd said, his voice hard and dripping with disdain. "Trey Potter. Son and heir to Potter's Pages, our number-one competitor, who's trying to buy us out."

I remember my heart thundering in my ears, humiliation flooding me as the world dropped beneath my feet. Trey had told me he was related to the Potters but never that he was the owner's son, never said anything about a hoped-for buyout. Neither had the Baileys, who by then confided in

Jonathan much more than me about the financial nuances of the business.

I stood under Jonathan Frost's disapproving glare, reeling as the pieces slipped into place—Trey's questions about the bookshop, about my relationship to the Baileys, his unwillingness to show his face here, his request that we keep our relationship private. Shocked, pride wounded, I lifted my chin defiantly and used every ounce of willpower not to cry as I gave Jonathan the silent treatment and stormed right by him.

That night, I confronted Trey and ended things with him. He'd pleaded with me to believe he loved me, that while he'd been tasked with "exploring a relationship with me for its strategic possibilities"—which, after talking with my best friends, I decoded to mean, "see if I could be romanced over to the Potters' side and persuaded to encourage the Baileys to sell"—he'd fallen for me in the process.

*I can't live without you, he'd said. You can't leave me. I'll never get over you.*

Here's the thing about reading romance: it's taught me an appreciation for a good grovel, but it's also taught me to recognize a toxic character when I see one. Trey, I realized, had toxic written all over him.

Since then, I've considered setting the record straight with Jonathan countless times, telling him he'd assumed the worst of me that day when he had no idea what I did or didn't know. That while I hate how he told me, I'm grateful he dropped that bomb. That because of his brutal honesty, I unearthed Trey's true motives, ended things with him, and told the Baileys exactly what had happened to be sure they knew my loyalty was wholly to them and this place.

But what stops me every time is this: discussing our personal lives isn't done in this battle for the bookshop, let alone confessing vulnerable feelings. That would require lowering our guard. In our never-ending battle for the upper hand, that's a risk I can't take.

In my most charitable moments toward Jonathan—and maybe they're also moments where I cared a *tiny* bit about his good opinion of me—I've hoped he'd put two and two together. That Jonathan would realize Trey was history, when months went on and no buyout happened, when my relationship with the Baileys remained warm and familial and there was no sign of my ex. Clearly, that's been too much to expect.

And now I know why. Jonathan Frost has only ever thought the worst of me. And maybe, deep down, I already knew that. But now that it's glaringly obvious, right in my face, the perverse delight I'll derive in proving him wrong far outweighs the legitimate vulnerability of what I'm about to admit. I can't do it anymore, can't take it a second longer, letting him be so damn smug and sure about exactly the kind of person he's decided I am.

So, staring up at Jonathan, I tell him, "It's definitely something Trey would do. Except he hasn't been my boyfriend since I broke up with him six months ago. You were, in fact, the one who enlightened me, Jonathan, but of course, you assumed I already knew about the buyout, instead of considering that since you got here, I've been shouldered out of important financial meetings, and that I had no clue. Thanks to you, I realized Trey was with me for my influence with the Baileys, hoping he could get me on his side and persuade them to accept the Potters' buyout offer."

The sting of embarrassment over what I've just said is swallowed up by glee as I watch color leech from Jonathan's face. His mouth parts. His hand drops from the flowers to the counter with a stunned *thunk*. I've rendered Jonathan Frost speechless.

Delighted, I flash him a satisfied smile. "Maybe it's time

to switch to police procedurals, Mr. Frost. Your sleuthing skills are slipping."

On that triumphant note, I pirouette away from the counter and sweep up my homemade decorations.

Time to make this place a winter wonderland.

# CHAPTER 2

## PLAYLIST: "GREENSLEEVES," MOUNTAIN MAN

Eight hours later, I'm greeted by twin shouts of "Welcome home!" as I shut the door behind me.

June and Eli, my best friends as well as roommates, are stationed in their positions when our free evenings line up—Eli on the sofa, waiting to share a weighted blanket, June, the solitary ruler on her recliner throne. Throwing a marshmallow at the TV, June *boo-hiss*es as Michael Cain's Ebenezer Scrooge walks on screen. The holiday movie marathon has commenced.

"Food," I mutter blearily, toeing off my boots. I tear away my winter gear and leave it behind me in a soggy trail through the foyer of our apartment.

"Soup's hot," Eli says.

"Good. I need to thaw."

I wander into the kitchen and ladle myself a bowl of Eli's glorious chicken soup, fighting a pang of blindsiding melancholy. June's unwashed to-go coffee mugs litter the counter beside Eli's cookbooks. Eli laughs at the movie as June gives Scrooge a colorful hand gesture. I shut my eyes and savor the moment, locking it away in my memories, because I know this roommate set-up won't last forever.

Since college, the three of us have lived together because it allowed us to save money in an expensive city and afford a nicer place than we could have otherwise rented on our own. But I know what's coming. Soon, Eli and his boyfriend, Luke, will get a place together; June will finally move closer to the hospital because she's tired of the long commute.

And I'll be solitary Gabriella, with her cat Gingerbread and her floor-to-ceiling stacks of romance novels. Which isn't a bad life, it's just...I'll miss them, and I suck at adjusting to change, and the truth is that while the holidays are my favorite time of year, it's not just because I love snow and peppermint-chocolate everything and sugar cookies and cele-bratory traditions—it's the *people* I share this time of year with who make it mean everything to me. It's our holiday movie marathon and baking my family's pizzelle recipe along-side Eli's sufganiyot. It's the three of us taking our annual stroll through the conservatory's Winter Wonderland display with boozy cider in our thermoses and June starting a tipsy snowball fight on our walk home.

What if it's our last holiday living together?

June catches me lost in my maudlin thoughts and frowns. "Everything okay?"

"Yep." I turn away so she can't see me mope. "How was work, you two?"

"Busy," they both answer.

That's about all I get from them when I ask about work, since it's client confidential. June's an ICU nurse, and Eli's a children's therapist.

"How about you?" June calls as I toast myself a piece of bread.

"Exhausting," I tell her, watching the opening of *The*

*Muppet Christmas Carol* on the TV. "I dealt with my own Scrooge all day."

Jonathan was surlier than normal as I decorated the bookshop and hummed along to my holiday playlist. While I decked the halls with homemade glittering clay and papier mâché snowflakes and dreidels, kinaras and Christmas trees, seven-star piñatas and menorahs and fire and light solstice symbols, I repeatedly caught him looking at me with that new, brow-furrowed, cryptic expression. And when it was time for him to leave—we alternate who stays until seven to close up—he stormed out without even his usual surly "Goodnight."

As I return to the living room, Eli whips back the blanket for me on the sofa. I land with an ungainly flop and just manage not to splash soup all over us.

"So you dealt with Mr. Scrooge," he says, "*and* it's the first of December. Meaning you decorated the bookstore today. That'll wear anyone out. How you do that by yourself is beyond me. You should hire some people to help."

"There's no money for that, El."

"That jerk she works with could help her," June mutters into her soup.

"Hah." I snort. "He'd never. Jonathan's such a grinch."

Pausing the movie, Eli says diplomatically, "Maybe the holidays are difficult for him."

June and I level him with a hard glare.

He lifts his free hand in surrender. "I'm just saying, for all sorts of valid reasons, not everyone loves the holidays."

"What's not to love? I work hard to include and represent all the winter holidays, to make sure anyone who visits Bailey's feels welcome and seen."

Eli settles the weighted blanket onto my lap. "And you do that beautifully. But following your logic, if we truly welcome everyone's celebration of the season, that includes welcoming even those who don't find it so celebratory."

I wrinkle my nose. "I don't like when you make sense."

"Would you leave your therapist hat in the office and stop being so compassionate?" June stretches out of her recliner and yanks the remote from his lap. "It's going to rub off on me."

"Yeah, El." I nudge him playfully with my foot. "Whose side are you on anyway? May I remind you that working with Jonathan Frost has shaved years off my life? That I've developed acid reflux since he came to the store?"

"Okay," June says, "the nurse in me must point out that your acid reflux would be way better controlled if you weren't a certified chocoholic. And if your diet wasn't ninety percent tomatoes."

"I'm half-Italian! These things cannot be helped."

June plops back into her recliner with the remote on a contented sigh. "Dietary choices aside, the guy is still a dick, and he certainly hasn't helped your GERD."

"Can I ask something?" Eli says.

"Fine," I grumble. "But make it quick. I want to watch Muppets dressed in Victorian clothes and forget about reality."

"Does Jonathan know you're on the spectrum?"

I fidget and stir my soup. "No."

"But the Baileys do," he says.

"Yes."

"Your point?" June asks, leveling him with one of her sharp, intimidating looks.

"What I'm getting at is, with the Baileys, Gabby, you're your authentic self, right?"

I nod.

"And not that I think you need to label yourself with folks to be your authentic self," he continues, "but I'm wondering if there's a reason the Baileys know and Jonathan doesn't. Are you your authentic self with *him*?"

I avoid Eli's eyes, staring into my soup as steam wafts off its surface. "I don't know. Mostly? I don't hide my sensory stuff, and I don't pretend to be anything other than who I am..."

"But," Eli says gently.

"But I haven't explained my social struggles, anything I'd convey when trying to form a friendship or relationship with someone, because...well, I had no plans on being friends or anything else with him."

"Why not?" Eli asks.

"He's just always been so...intimidating and arrogant and..."

*And you've had a chip on your shoulder since the day you met him, the angel on my shoulder chides, when you saw him as the human embodiment of every aptitude that makes you feel inadequate.*

The devil on my other side says nothing—just maneuvers her pitchfork, revealing an extendable handle that makes it long enough to poke the angel off my shoulder and send her into a screaming freefall.

I think I'm coming unhinged.

"Gabby?" Eli's voice snaps me out of my angel-devil dilemma. "I understand your logic, and you know I'll always respect your decision on this. That said, do you see how it might be better between you two if he knew the things he does that confuse you and make communication difficult and push your buttons?"

"But then..." I swallow nervously, licking my lips. "But then he'd know my soft spot. And I wouldn't know his."

The devil on my shoulder nods in agreement.

"Or he might follow suit and show you his soft spot, too," Eli counters. "And then you'd have shared vulnerability together. You might even become friends."

June gives him another sharp look. Some sort of neurotypical eye conversation happens.

"Hey." I snap my fingers. "Stop talking around me."

"Eli reads too many romance novels," June says.

I frown between them. I read and sell romance novels for a living and I'm not making the connection. "Huh?"

"I just wonder if he likes you," Eli says, carefully. "But because he doesn't know how you tick, he's blown it to hell so far in showing you he cares."

I stare at him, stunned. A bubble of silence swells in the room until I burst it with laughter. I laugh so hard, my sides hurt and there are tears streaming down my face. "Oh God. That's good."

Eli's not laughing. "I'm serious."

"I'm unimpressed," June says. "Even if he does 'like' her, being a dick is an ass-backwards, misogynistically regressive way of showing it."

"There's no chance," I tell them. "Especially considering that, up until today, he clearly thought I was still dating the enemy."

"But you broke up with Trey as soon as you found out who he really was," Eli says.

June blinks at me in confusion. "So why did the asshole think you two were still dating?"

"I wasn't giving him a relationship report, and while I thought it was pretty obvious Trey was out of the picture, I guess Jonathan assumed we were still together and that I'd just become more discreet about it."

Eli scooches closer on the sofa. "Okay, but how did he learn that you broke up?"

I stare longingly at the movie, paused on screen. "Are we ever going to see a ghost scare the shit out of Michael Cain?"

"After you clear this up," Eli says.

Sighing, I set down my soup and flop back on the sofa.

"Trey sent a grotesquely expensive holiday bouquet to the shop this morning with a note that said, and I quote, 'All I want for Christmas is you.'"

"Ewww." June grimaces. "What a creep. How many different numbers of his have you blocked?"

"Five. Thought I made myself pretty clear. So this bouquet came," I tell them, "Jonathan saw the note, and then he gave me shit about my boyfriend not being considerate enough to order a low-fragrance bouquet. That's when I told him I didn't have a boyfriend anymore."

Eli sits back, stroking his jaw. "And how did Jonathan respond to that?"

I stretch toward June's recliner and hit play on the remote in her hand. "He turned the color of slushy street snow after a long day of traffic and gaped like a broken nutcracker. It was *delightful*."

June's eyes widen. Eli flashes her a slow, smug smile, but I hardly notice.

"Now can we please watch *The Muppet Christmas Carol*?" I ask them, propping my feet on Eli's lap. "I need at least one Scrooge in my life to get what's coming to him."

After the movie, I shower, then change into my favorite snowflake-print pajamas. Hair wrapped in a T-shirt to dry my curls and humming "Greensleeves," I waltz into my bedroom. Gingerbread, my orange tabby cat, snoozes, draped like a starfish on my bouncy ball chair. I pluck her off before I sit in her place, then settle her on my lap.

Smiling at the sound and feel of her rumbling purr as she settles back to sleep, I power on my laptop and bring the screen to life.

A photo of June, Eli, and me, huddled close, fills the

screen. Eli grins, auburn ringlets falling over his eyes, which are squinted shut because the man can't help but blink when his picture is taken. Glossy chin-length black hair, crinkled nose, wide smile, June has her arms hooked around our necks, temple to temple with Eli, smooshing my curls to my head as I kiss her cheek. Snow dusts our heads like confectioner's sugar, the conservatory's Winter Wonderland display a tapestry of intricate twinkling lights behind us.

Looking at the photo, I'm overwhelmed with gratitude—for loving parents who are good people, friends who are the siblings I never had, a faithful feline pet, a city that feels like home, a job that I love run by people I love even more. I have so much to be thankful for. And if my only true burden in this life—even if he is a very large, surly burden—is Jonathan Frost, I guess I can deal with that.

"Hey."

I spin around to face June standing on the threshold of my room.

"You okay?" she asks. "I know we got a little intense back there about the work nemesis situation. I'm just protective of you. And Eli's a hopeless romantic."

"I know." I smile. "I love you both for it. I'm fine. Just tired."

She nods. "All right. Don't stay up too late talking to Mr. Reddit."

I roll my eyes. "Yes, Mom."

Eli and June have admitted they don't quite understand why I talk daily with someone I've never met, whose real name I don't know, whose personal life I don't know much about either, except that—smallest of worlds—we've figured out we live in the same city.

I could try to explain my relationship with Mr. Reddit, as June and Eli named him, but I'm protective of how great talking to him makes me feel. Behind the safety of a screen,

I'm my most sophisticated self—articulate, witty, sharp. Mr. Reddit hasn't seen me struggle to read his facial expressions or observed how often I wear my noise-cancelling headphones or learned how anxious I get when life veers off my routine. And listen, I love myself for who I am, every part of me, the parts that fit easily in this world and the parts that don't, but it's a whole other thing to ask someone *else* to love me for all of those parts, too.

I don't show Mr. Reddit those parts that don't fit so well, and in doing so, I don't risk him rejecting them, either.

That's the truth of why I don't tell June and Eli more. I know how they'd see it. Eli would encourage me to embrace vulnerability. June would say the person who deserves me will be wild about *all* of me, otherwise they can fuck the fuck off.

And my friends would be right. But it's easy for them to say. They don't understand what pursuing friendship and romance is like for me, how being autistic and demisexual means not just the exposure of myself, like it is for anyone when they meet people and try to forge a connection, but weighing when and how to trust someone with the truth of who I am, a truth that's not always been met with understanding or acceptance or kindness.

So I've kept Mr. Reddit to myself since we met, a little over a year ago on a bookish Reddit thread that got real heated when a guy started mansplaining George Orwell's *1984*, and another someone—that would be me—patiently, logically explained how wrong he was.

It went south fast. The guy started calling me nasty names.

And then in came What_The_Charles_Dickens like a total badass, cutting him off at the rhetorical knees. I mean, I didn't *need* a Reddit knight in shining armor, but I wasn't opposed to one. And thus began our online bookish friendship.

By unspoken agreement, What_The_Charles_Dickens, aka Mr. Reddit, and I talk only in the evenings on a chat plat-form, Telegram, that requires you to register with your phone number but allows you to show only your username. Knowing my propensity to hyper-focus, bordering on obsess, I've purposefully not downloaded the Telegram app on my phone, meaning I can only chat with him when I'm home on my computer.

Each night, after catching up with June and/or Eli, depending on their work schedules, then dinner and a shower, I settle in at my desk, Gingerbread on my lap, and wind down the day talking with Mr. Reddit. I'm a creature of habit, and he's become a vital part of my routine. That's why when I turn back to the screen and open up my Telegram desktop chat, my heart sinks. There's no new message.

It's rare that Mr. Reddit doesn't leave a message for me. Since we started talking, it's happened twice, and both times he later explained he'd been sick and unable to write.

I take a deep breath, try to exhale my disappointment, and scroll through yesterday evening's chat between formerly What_The_Charles_Dickens, who switched his username to Mr. Reddit since I slipped about it being my roommate's nickname for him, and MargaretCATwood, or as Mr. Reddit dubbed me, MCAT, because I can't help myself. I start with his message that was waiting for me when I sat down last night.

**MR. REDDIT:** Can we talk about how Marianne Dash-wood needs some deep-breathing exercises?

**MCAT:** She's a hopeless romantic. She's supposed to come across as a little dramatic.

He's reading Jane Austen's *Sense and Sensibility*, because I gave him hell for only having read *Pride and Prejudice*.

**MR. REDDIT:** A *little* dramatic? "It is not time or opportunity that is to determine intimacy; it is disposition alone. Seven years would be insufficient to make some people acquainted with each other, and seven days are more than enough for others." Seriously? Seven days "to determine intimacy"? With that sage wisdom guiding her romantic life, not gonna lie, I'm guessing Marianne falls for a jerk.

**MCAT:** I mean, yes, she falls for a guy who turns out to be a cad. But it's not all on her! He sweeps her off her feet and conveniently neglects to tell her he's broke and needs to marry an heiress, which Marianne definitely isn't. She gets her heart broken, so be nice to her.

**MR. REDDIT:** SPOILERS!

**MCAT:** Oh come on, she's the hopeless romantic in the novel. You knew Austen was going to crush her soul.

**MR. REDDIT:** SPOILERS, CATWOOD.

**MCAT:** I'm sorry!

**MR. REDDIT:** Sure you are.

**MCAT:** I am! I didn't think I was in spoiler territory. I thought it was obvious.

**MR. REDDIT:** It's anything but obvious! I'm reading a romance, expecting the guy she's falling for to be a keeper, not a heartbreaker.

Even though I'm rereading it, I gasp again. Gingerbread blinks up at me sleepily and rolls onto her back. Rubbing her tummy, I sigh dramatically and shake my head. "Don't worry, Gingerbread, I showed him the error of his ways."

**MCAT:** Mr. Reddit. Austen's stories are often romantic, but they're not exactly romances in the modern sense. They're novels of manners first and foremost.

**MR. REDDIT:** Wow. I thought Austen was one of the earliest and most influential romance novelists.

**MCAT:** Well her work's been romanticized by popular culture, made into movies that emphasize the romantic aspects. And Pride and Prejudice is absolutely swoony as hell, I can't argue with that. Her other novels have some incredibly romantic storylines and moments, too. She's just…not necessarily a romance novelist in the full sense of the genre. Much as I adore Austen, there's so much more to romance, and I wish more people knew that.

**MR. REDDIT:** I wish I'd known, too. Because foolishly I was expecting a HAPPILY EVER AFTER.

**MCAT:** Well, at least you know *that* criteria for romance —the HEA.

**MR. REDDIT:** I know we talk about a lot of different books, but I get the feeling romance is your favorite genre. Am I right?

**MCAT:** Definitely. It's all I can read lately—well, besides buddy-rereading Austen with you.

Once upon a time I read a variety of fiction, but the past few months, it's only been romance. After dueling with Jonathan Bah-Humbug Frost all day, I need assholes to get their comeuppance and happy endings only. I also sell a ton of romance at the bookstore. I'm passionate about getting people to challenge those uncharitable stereotypes about the genre and give it a try. I was prepared for Mr. Reddit to display some of those prejudices, too.

But he didn't.

A smile warms my face as I read his response. Last night, it made me light up like the family Christmas tree after Dad's thrown every single light on that sucker that he can. And tonight, it makes me glow all over again.

**MR. REDDIT:** Alright, then CATwood. Tell me what to read.

**MCAT:** Seriously? You'll read a romance novel?

**MR. REDDIT:** I will. Where should I start?

I scroll through the list of recommendations I gave him (I may or may not have gotten a little carried away and listed my very favorites in order, but I'm a bookseller—recommending books is my joy!). When I get to the end of our chat, with Mr. Reddit's usual *Sleep tight, MCAT*, I bite my lip and war with myself. My fingers hover over the keys, aching to type what

I've debated writing so many times the past few months, since my mind started wondering, *What if?*

What if my online friendship with Mr. Reddit became a real-life friendship? And then, what if, one day, it became something more? That hope—for the possibility of more with him—has crept up on me gradually since I broke up with Trey.

Knowing how I work, it hasn't been entirely surprising, after a year of talking daily with Mr. Reddit and growing so close, that some nights, when the rare wave of longing washed over me, it's been the thought of him that got me off —the warmth that I imagined filling his voice, the thoughtfulness guiding his every question and curiosity about my answers.

Each time it happens, I feel a little more ready to ask him: *Do you think we should meet?*

But as I stare at my screen, my courage fails me, especially in light of his silence tonight. What if he only wants to be my friend? What if I'd ruin this good, safe, comforting connection we have by asking to explore our potential to become more?

So in the end, I don't type what I want. I don't dare risk confessing what Marianne does—that poor, hopeless romantic:

*"If I could but know his heart, everything would become easy."*

# CHAPTER 3

On may walk to work, I manifest a positive attitude. Today is going to be better. Even though I tossed and turned, worried about Mr. Reddit and why he hadn't messaged, and then, when I turned to a historical romance audiobook like usual to mellow me out until sleep kicked in, I had the disturbing experience of reading a book whose hero was a dead-ringer for Jonathan Frost.

As I listened from the heroine's perspective, my imagination refused to conjure anyone but him—this grumpy, no-smiles jerk of a hero who smelled like wintry-forests Jonathan and sounded like gruff, surly Jonathan and looked like broad, muscly Jonathan.

Even worse, while still listening to my romance audiobook, I finally fell asleep. That's when my dreams took over.

Caught in a weird limbo of a Regency England romance novel filtering through my headphones and the wicked work of my subconscious, I was a feisty bluestocking hiding from the crushed ballroom in her family's library with a penny dreadful. Jonathan was the serious, broody, duke whose radically favorable views on industrialization scandalized the other gentry, even though their agricultural wealth was fast dying, so he came slinking into that same library I was hiding in to escape his intransigent aristocratic peers and find himself a bracing pour of my father's finest single-malt whiskey.

But instead he found me. And asked what I was reading. Which, hello, with me, that's how you hop in the fast lane on the expressway to friendship: talk to me about books. One thing led to another. Banter was bantered. Bluestocking Gabby was playful rather than pissy. Ducal Jonathan was curious as opposed to cantankerous. Instead of our dynamic's real life hostility, we were *combustible*.

Off came cravat and corset, petticoats and placket, and then it was his big, strong body heavy over mine, his stern mouth whispering filthy things in my ear as he made me writhe and gasp beneath him. It was so vivid, a fire roaring, soft abandoned clothes beneath my back, as he filled me, touched me, coaxing me expertly to pleasure, like he'd mapped every inch of me and knew exactly how to drive me wild—

A horn blares, wrenching me from my thoughts. I've walked into the middle of oncoming traffic, which has a green light.

"Watch where you're going!" a cab driver yells.

Thankfully their voice and interspersed honking is muffled by my noise-cancelling headphone earmuffs. Loud sounds like that hurt my brain. I lift my hand in apology and hurry across the street. "Sorry!"

Speeding up, I hustle along the sidewalk. I'm running late *again* because I woke up so flustered from my dream, so turned on I could barely put my clothes on right. Then I walked out the door without my bag before I realized I hadn't put on my boots. I'm a mess.

And I'm having a crisis. Because this isn't how attraction works for me—I desire people I feel close to, connected with. Who I like. I don't *like* Jonathan.

*But is liking really what you need? the devil on my shoulder whispers. Or is it closeness? A bond? You are bonded with him, aren't you?*

*More like trapped, the angel on my other side reminds me. Tangled. Ensnared. These are not good things.*

The angel's right, but the devil's not wrong either. Jonathan and I *are* bonded. Yes, it's a twisty bond, united in our love of the bookstore but divided by how to manage it, opposite personalities who can't stand each other yet in many ways know each other inside out, but that doesn't make it any less of a bond. And, God, the sheer absurd amount of time we've spent together, just the two of us in the bookshop, bickering and provoking each other. How many hours did Jonathan say it was? Over two thousand?

That's a lot. Too much. It's clearly getting to me, tricking my body into fantasizing about the last thing I should want from someone who I cannot stand.

*There's a reason you're fantasizing about him, the devil whispers. Don't you want to figure that out?*

*The angel tsks primly, shaking her head. She used to fantasize about Mr. Reddit. That's who she's supposed to fantasize about—*

"Argh!" I throw up my hands and stomp down the sidewalk. I don't have time for these angel-devil debates. I don't even have time to get myself a peppermint hot cocoa. Which means my routine is off, I'm hungry and sugar-deprived, and I'm sorely lacking in seasonal beverage goodness.

Just as my mood is really heading south, my headphones start to play a jazzy version of "Sleigh Ride" sung by Ella

Fitzgerald (of course), and I can't help but smile just a little, the sudden happiness the music brings reminding me how I started this walk to work: committed to staying positive. So I pep-talk myself as I wrap up my walk to the store. Today is going to be better! Work is going to be great! The bookshop is decorated beautifully for the holidays; I have a whole month of fun, festive activities to draw crowds, sell books, and spread cheer. And no traumatically sexual dream about Jonathan Frost in skin-tight breeches is going to bring me down.

Opening the door to the bookshop, which is unlocked like it always is because Jonathan's always there first, I feel a surge of joy as I drink in the space.

Polished, glowing wood floors and columns, built-in bookshelves, every gorgeous beam curved along the vaulted ceilings. Row after colorful row of book spines filling shelves and stacked on wood tables, a treasure chest of bookish gems. The gas fireplace dances with cheery flames beneath the mantel, which I decorated with oversized jewel-tone ornaments, glittering fake snow, and soft pine boughs. All across the ceiling hang my homemade sparkling papier mâché and clay baked decorations that honor the winter holidays, swirls of white, gold, and silver ribbon threaded among them and reflecting the morning light like sunrise mirrored on a frozen pond.

The sight before me, the comforting smell of books mingling with fresh-cut evergreens, wraps me in a blanket of festive bliss.

Which is why it hurts all the worse when I'm hit with a one-two punch of recognition and dread. It's not Jonathan Frost and his arctic glare greeting me, reminding me I'm three minutes late. It's the Baileys, smiling warmly. The owners. Who are rarely here, and never first thing in the morning.

"Morning, dear!" Mrs. Bailey calls from the far end of the store.

Mr. Bailey strolls my way on a soft smile and waves me in. "Come in, Gabby."

He's wearing a cheery matching plaid bow tie and suspenders that coordinate with Mrs. Bailey's skirt. They're so precious, it makes a lump form in my throat. These people matter to me—their store and this job matter to me. And something's wrong. I know it.

Rounding the large central display table, Mrs. Bailey wraps me in a hug. "Happy holidays, dear! The store looks gorgeous..." She pulls back, examining me as I try to smile back at her. "What's the matter?"

"That's what *I* want to know."

Her smile falters a little. "Oh, Gabby, don't worry. It's just a little business chat. Everything will be fine."

Mr. Bailey rubs his forehead and mutters to himself, "Just a little business chat."

"Relax, George. Don't get your suspenders in a twist." Mrs. Bailey pats him gently on the arm, then turns back to me. "Gabby, go ahead and get unbundled there, then let's have a seat around the table in the back room. Jonathan just called and said he'll be here in a minute."

"He's expecting you?" My voice comes out a squeak.

Mrs. Bailey settles into a chair at one end of the table and frowns up at me. "I told Jonathan about the meeting last week when I stopped by shortly before he closed up. He said he'd pass along the information to you. Didn't he?"

Some other bosses might use modern methods of communication like email or text messaging, or hell, even a call, but the Baileys are blatant technophobes. They don't even have cell phones. I learn things from them in person, or I don't learn them at all. Jonathan's aware of this. It drives him up the wall. Apparently, not so much that he doesn't mind using it to his advantage, though.

Wow. I knew he was a jerk, but this is a new low.

While a tiny part of me is actually relieved I haven't had this hanging over my head for a week, seeing as my anxiety thrives in the soil of unknowns and I'd have spent the past seven days giving myself an ulcer, applying for unemployment, and pointlessly rearranging the bookshelves, I'm still overwhelmingly angry.

Because *Jonathan* doesn't know that he spared me a week of anxiety.

He doesn't know that, ideally, I'd have found out, say, a day in advance, given myself twenty-four hours to catastrophize and brace myself for the worst. He wasn't trying to protect me from my mind's talent for obsessive worrying. No, he kept this meeting from me so he'd have the upper hand. And I'm not letting that happen. Which means, I'm not telling the Baileys that no, Jonathan did *not* apprise me of this meeting, when it would amount to confessing I'm totally unprepared.

"Ohhhh," I lie, unwinding my scarf, then shrugging off my coat. "*That* meeting. Of course. I just got my days switched around."

Mrs. Bailey seems to buy it. "Understandable. I get so turned around this time of year. There's too much going on!"

Smiling tightly, I glance up at the clock. Jonathan's now ten minutes late. He's never late. "So...where *is* Jonathan?"

"Here."

I jump a foot in the air and clutch my chest over my pounding heart. I try to keep my gaze down, but I can't seem to stop it from trailing up his body. My cheeks heat. After that steamy romance-audiobook-turned-dream last night, I can barely look at him. Except I kind of can't *stop* looking at him.

His dark wavy hair is windblown. His pale green eyes glitter like frost-kissed pines. A splash of pink warms his sharp cheekbones, stung by the cold air, and he's holding a to-go beverage carrier. Someone so evil should not be this hot. I can't believe I had a sex dream about him. I want to bleach the memory from my brain.

"Gabriella."

My eyes snap up and meet his. "What?"

He arches an eyebrow. "Could I get by?"

"Oh! Right." I debate tripping him as payback for the meeting sabotage but think better of doing that in front of the Baileys. Instead, I step back and lean against the counter so he can enter the break room kitchenette, my mind spinning with possibilities of how I can make him suffer later.

Jonathan walks past me, the scent of peppermint and chocolate wafting from one of the cups he's holding. That asshole. He got me my drink. He probably put arsenic in it.

My gaze follows him as he sets the hot beverages on the table and exchanges morning greetings with the Baileys. As Mrs. Bailey eases each cup from the carrier, Jonathan turns and shrugs off his coat. The wintry-woods scent of his body hits me, jarring new memories from my twisted dream last night—strong hands gripping my waist, flipping me over, lifting my hips until I'm on my knees. A rough palm sliding up my back, fingers curling around my hair, smoothing it from my face. Lips trailing down my spine, my ass, lower, then *lower*—

I scrunch my eyes shut and grip the counter, steadying myself against the heat flooding my body.

"All right, Gabriella?" Jonathan's voice is rougher this morning, how I imagine it is right when he wakes up.

Not that I've imagined that in any great detail—what that body of his looks like in morning sunlight, winter-white bedsheets pooled low around his hips. That shape of his severe mouth softened in a sleepy smile. His bare chest expanding when he stretches pleasurably and groans awake.

Nope. Never thought about that. Definitely not thinking about it now that I know what a conniving, sabotaging son of a—

"Gabriella."

My eyes snap open and meet his, a fresh wave of lust cresting inside me. This is so unfair. Here I am, about to have A Very Serious Business Meeting with my bosses and professional nemesis who I had a white-hot, unresolved (if you know what I'm saying) dream about. I'm unprepared and flustered and horny, and here's Jonathan with hot beverages for everyone, cool as a fucking cucumber.

I should be repulsed, but instead my breasts are tender and there's a deep warm ache between my legs. He should look like a lump of grumpy coal, with that stern expression, his ink-black sweater, and charcoal trousers, but instead Jonathan Frost looks like sex and smoke and a starless night sky.

I hate him for it.

"What do you want?" I hiss.

He tips his head, scanning my face. "I asked if you're all right."

Like he cares. It's all part of his act in front of the Baileys.

I tip my chin and throw back my shoulders. "Why wouldn't I be?"

His eyes search mine. I stare right back.

"Ready to start?" Mrs. Bailey calls.

Jonathan blinks, then turns her way. "Absolutely."

"Yep!" It comes out thin and pinched. I clear my throat, pressing a cool hand to my cheek as I follow Jonathan to the table.

Just before I can reach for the chair in front of me, Jonathan's hand closes around it and drags it out. Clearly another part of his gentlemanly act for the Baileys. I glare and beam him a telepathic warning: *I see right through you.*

Jonathan arches an eyebrow. The corner of his mouth tips in wry amusement as he beams back a nonchalant *Sure you do.*

On a huff, I sit. He slides my chair forward. And then he rounds the table, lowering himself to the seat across from me.

Mrs. Bailey slides a cup my way. "This should put a smile on your lovely face, my dear."

"Ah, great. Thanks." I pop off the lid, then breathe in. I'm deeply sensitive to smell, and I know *exactly* what my perfect peppermint hot cocoa smells like—double shots of peppermint, two-percent milk, extra whip, and chocolate drizzle.

This is it.

How does Jonathan know exactly how I drink it? And why don't I smell rat poison? Does cyanide have an odor?

For a moment, everything's quiet. Mr. Bailey sips an uncomplicated latte. Mrs. Bailey sips hers, too, though her cup reeks of cinnamon and nutmeg. They both look at me expectantly.

Right. I've been given something. Politeness is called for. Worse, gratitude.

If it's not the poison in my drink, it's what I'm about to do that's going to kill me, but I swallow my pride, bare a grimacing smile, and say between clenched teeth, "Thank you, Jonathan, for my peppermint hot cocoa."

He lifts the lid on his black coffee, then meets my gaze, arching an eyebrow as he takes a long, slow drink. His tongue darts out as he licks a fleck of coffee from his bottom lip. My thighs pin together beneath the table.

"You're welcome, Gabriella."

An electric *zing* arcs through the air, as if the universe was about as prepared for a civil exchange between us as it is for nuclear fusion. Jonathan's mouth tips, the faintest lift at the corner, like he's read my mind and found this moment just as ironically amusing.

"So." Mrs. Bailey wraps her hands around her cup. "Thank you for gathering. What do you want first—the good news or the bad?"

"Bad," Jonathan tells her, as I say, "Good."

Mr. Bailey scrubs his face and sighs.

"Fine," I mutter, before taking a long swig of perfect peppermint hot cocoa to console myself. I'm too desperate for sugar to worry if it's about to kill me. "Just lower the boom."

"Take it away, dear," Mrs. Bailey tells her husband.

Mr. Bailey gives her a disgruntled look, then says, "As we expected, the arrival of a Potter's Pages to the neighborhood two years ago has undeniably led to decreased profits. Their competitive pricing and massive inventory was bad enough, but their online store, particularly e-books...it's become impossible to compete with."

Jonathan's gaze snaps between the Baileys with a kind of laser-focused intensity that I have no idea what to make of. What am I missing?

Silence stretches between the four of us, and I take the moment to examine Jonathan for some clue as to what's going on. Hands folded on the table like a boardroom executive, back straight, ink-black cashmere sweater clinging to his broad shoulders and chest like it was poured over him, he looks straight out of those 500-page fantasy romances that I devour, like the villain who turns out to be the hero. Except this is reality—here, the villain's the villain.

"Historically," Jonathan says, breaking the silence, "Bailey's hasn't *tried* to compete with a chain bookstore strategy. We've focused on providing a curated, boutique in-person experience because we have a different target demographic and customer base than Potter's Pages. Are you saying..." he glances my way, then back to them, "that you'd consider altering that approach?"

"I'm open to it," Mrs. Bailey says carefully, meeting her husband's eye. Mr. Bailey nods in agreement. "Bottom line is, we need more customers and more sales to offset what we've lost to Potter's. If not, we'll have to take a long, hard look at the bookshop's future and whether we open our doors again after the new year."

My world tips sideways. I clutch my cup so hard, I expect hot cocoa to geyser up to the ceiling.

"We'll have to get creative," she continues, "about how we broaden our reach, and we need record high sales this month. And, of course, we'll make some more cuts in expenses."

Getting creative? That's my wheelhouse. My mind whirs with possibilities. A big sale right before we close, live music, holiday crafts, pastries, hot beverages. Might get a bit messy, but that's what all-purpose cleaner is for. Maybe a book club would draw some new customers? I'm not great at group settings, but if it's only once a month and everyone buys the book from us, it could be worth it.

Of course, just when my ideas are really picking up steam, Jonathan crushes them like a number-crunching piano fallen from the sky.

"Due respect," he says, a deep furrow in his brow, "there *are* no expenses left to cut. The past year, I've made sure we're as lean as possible, trimmed our overhead every place I could. Outside of management, we're down to one part-time employee—well, we were, until he quit, and now it's just—"

"Us," I say faintly.

My heart plummets. When it comes to cutting expenses, all that's left to cut is...one of us. My worst nightmare just came true.

Mrs. Bailey sighs and sips her spiced latte. "That's the bad news. During an already stressful, demanding time of year, we're tasking you with even more so the place can stay open for years to come, Potter's Pages be damned."

"And...the good news?" I ask weakly.

"The good news..." Mrs. Bailey smiles between us. "I have every faith your efforts will be a success."

# CHAPTER 4

PLAYLIST: "LITTLE JACK FROST, GET
LOST," BING CROSBY & PEGGY LEE

"**W**ell, that was grim," I say through a smile, waving goodbye to the Baileys.

Jonathan stands beside me, arms folded across his chest, as we watch their cab pull out into snowy traffic. He says nothing, but I see those gears turning in his head. As if he's sensed me watching him, his pale green eyes snap my way. He stares at me for a long minute, softly falling snow and the slushy sound of tires rolling down the road filling the silence between us, stoic and chilly as ever.

How can he be so calm right now? Oh, that's right. He saw this meeting coming. Unlike me, he hasn't had the occupational rug pulled out from underneath him.

Finally free to carry out my revenge, I start with something that's guaranteed to piss him off. It has every other time I've done it. Smiling up at Jonathan, I start to hum.

*Little Jack Frost, get lost, get lost!*

His eyes narrow. His jaw ticks. God, it's satisfying.

"Too bad you don't go by Jack," I tell him, doing a little jazz square before I repeat the refrain. "I mean come on. Jack Frost? Does it get any better than that?"

Muttering to himself, he wrenches open the door and herds me across the threshold.

I don't like being corralled, but I'm not eager to stand out in the cold any longer than I have to in only a knee-length rose-pink sweater dress and no jacket. I dart inside, shivering as the store's heat envelops me. Then I turn to face Jonathan as he shuts the door and locks it, a bitter reminder that I'm stuck here with him in already strained professional circumstances that just took a turn for the worse.

"You know what this means," I tell him. "What the Baileys said."

Strolling past me, he sweeps up a stack of holiday romances that I set on the feature table and tucks them under his arm. "It means this independent bookstore is on the brink of financial collapse after years hemorrhaging money via outdated business methods, a deplorably inefficient HVAC system, zero online presence, and a flagrant disregard for competitive pricing."

"Well, yeah, but that's not what I meant."

He stops and turns, cool wintergreen eyes landing on me. "Then what *did* you mean, Gabriella?"

His sharp, condescending tone pops the lid off my pressure-cooker anger. Fuming, I close the distance between us and wrench the holiday romances from his grip, backtracking to the feature table. "Like you don't know what they were saying when they talked about cutting expenses. Unless a financial miracle happens, one of us isn't making it to the new year."

Jonathan sweeps up a stack of the wintertime paranormal thriller that just came out and drops it on the feature table with a thud, knocking over my holiday romances.

"Of course they're saying that," he snaps. "I've known that since I started, Gabriella. I've been planning for it since day one."

I angrily stack up the romances again, setting them in the front and shoving his winter thriller toward the back. "How nice for you, Jonathan. Some of us, however, have been too focused on our daily duties at the bookshop to spend time calculating professional sabotage."

"Ah, right," he says coolly. "Of course. I'm the hard-ass evil capitalist who came in and cruelly made a business efficient, while you're the innocent victim of my ruthless machinations, who never once wished me gone, whose love of books and whose gorgeous smiles for dwindling customers was magically going to keep things afloat."

My hands turn to fists.

"I'll admit this much," he says, his voice cold and deceptively soft. "I'm cerebral and strategic, Gabriella. I anticipated everything said in today's meeting. But spare us both the bullshit that I'm the only one who's had a less than forthright agenda since the day I was hired."

"Says the guy who kept this meeting from me!"

He shuts his eyes and grits his teeth. He knows he's busted. "I *meant* to tell you. I swear."

"Oh yeah?" I fold my arms across my chest. "When?"

"Yesterday, but—" He clears his throat. "Yesterday threw me off, and I forgot. I had every intention of telling you this morning, the moment you got here. But then the Baileys—for the first time ever and in the worst timing ever—got here early, and then I got delayed because that damn coffee shop that makes your fancy peppermint chocolate milk—"

"Hot cocoa!"

"Same thing! They messed up your order, so I had them make it again, and when I got here, I was too late. I could see it as you glared daggers at me. You'd already decided I left you in the dark on purpose."

"You've known for a *week*," I fire back. "Why did you wait until the last minute?"

He scrubs his face. "I guarantee you, Gabriella, if I explained myself, you wouldn't believe me."

I glare up at him. "Got me all figured out, have you?"

"Like you aren't just as guilty of that mindset?" He stares down at me, jaw clenched. "You think you've got me all figured out, too. And you can't stand me for it."

"I...resent you," I admit, hating how my voice wavers.

He arches an eyebrow. "That much is clear."

"You make me feel inadequate," I tell him through the lump in my throat. I blink away tears. "When they hired you, all I could think was you're here because I'm not good enough."

His expression falters. He opens his mouth like he's going to say something, but he's not fast enough. I'm on a roll.

"I'll admit that I have, at times, been petulant about your condescending, solitary reign of budget-cutting terror, Mr. Frost, but I've spent enough of my life being looked down on and dismissed, and I'm not doing that anymore. I have every right to stick up for myself."

He looks stricken now, his eyes darting between mine. He takes a step closer. I step back and bump into a table of books, sending a stack cascading to the ground. "Gabriella—"

"I love this place. With my whole heart," I whisper, the fire inside me burning brighter. "And we have three and a half weeks to save it." Pushing off the table, I step into his space, until I'm reminded that while I'm tall, Jonathan's much taller. Our chests brush. Our eyes meet. "Three and a half weeks until the shop closes for the year. Barring a financial miracle, expense cuts will come. One of us will have to leave Bailey's."

His eyes search mine for a charged, silent moment. "It's that simple?" he says.

"It's that *grim*. You heard them. You know the numbers even better than me."

"I do." Jonathan stares down at me, fierce, unblinking.

45

"And I'm not giving up that easily. I'm not walking away without fighting for this, Gabriella."

I glare up at him. "I anticipated that. So here's how it'll be decided. Whoever sells the most books this month, that's who gets to stay."

He's silent for a long, tense moment. And when he speaks, his voice is flat and cold. "That's the only way you can see it."

"I'll concede raw book sales isn't the most comprehensive measure of managerial competency, but let's face it, from here on out, the winner will be leveraging what the other has brought to the place. Without me, you'd have a bookstore frozen in 1988. Thanks to years of my influence, you have a beautiful space to welcome and sell to your customers, brimming with inviting, personal touches; an accessible, intuitive layout by genre and subgenre; and an entire calendar year of already-scheduled events and book signings. Thanks to *me*."

"And thanks to *me*," he says, "you have an HVAC system that isn't singlehandedly melting the polar ice caps, costing a small nation's GDP in a utility bill and driving customers away with its inability to regulate temperature; a data-driven inventory expansion strategized by key segment customers; oh, and of course, that minor detail, a payment and book-keeping system that belongs in the twenty-first century."

I sniff. "It wasn't that bad."

"The air-conditioning blew a fuse twice a week, the radiators were a ticking time bomb, our inventory had no basis in consumer analytics, and that ancient bronze abacus you called an 'antique' was both inefficient and the culprit for countless mischarges."

I gasp. "Gilda. I miss her."

"Gilda." He glances up at the ceiling, as if in a plea to God for patience. "You were manually entering prices on a Victorian cash register."

"A *gilded* Victorian cash register. Gilda had character!"

"She caused an IRS audit!"

We glower at each other. Our faces are dangerously close. Shit, he smells good. Like evergreens and winter air and woodsmoke. I feel an embarrassing rush of heat stain my cheeks.

Jonathan's gaze travels my face—my chin defiantly tipped up, my tell-tale flush. His jaw ticks. His brow furrows. Silence stretches, raw and taut, between us.

"Well?" I ask, desperate for this to end, for space from him, because I'm livid and I'm also unspeakably aroused. Everything I fantasized last night, everything I'm feeling now —his heat, his scent, the raw energy thrumming between us, makes me want to wrap my legs around his waist and drag his mouth down to mine until we hate-kiss so hard, we black out from lack of oxygen.

I shut my eyes, mentally cutting the cord between heavenly Fantasy Jonathan and his hellish reality. "You're in my personal space."

"You started it," he points out.

I open my mouth. Then shut it. He's right, I did. "Fine. Well, I'm done with personal-space time now."

He's a foot away from me in one smooth step. "Better?"

"Much." I push away from the table and dust myself off. "Now what do you have to say about my terms, Mr. Frost?"

He folds his arms across his chest and stares down at me. "Just book sales?"

"Just book sales," I confirm.

Damn him and that condescending arched eyebrow. "You do remember some of the best psychological thrillers in recent memory came out this year or are about to be released."

"Four words for you, Mr. Frost: children's books and holiday romances."

"Technically, that's five—"

I stomp my foot. "You know what I mean! Now answer me already, do you accept these terms or not?"

Tense silence stretches between us, punctured only by the wall-mounted clock ticking down the minutes left in this miserable merry-go-round of our professional enmity.

Finally he says, "I accept them."

"Excellent." With a disingenuous smile, I slip by him and return to my half-destroyed display of holiday romances.

"On one condition."

Grinding my teeth, I glare at him over my shoulder. "What?"

Jonathan leans against one of the polished wood columns that soars up to the store's vaulted ceiling and watches me, ankles crossed, hands in his pockets. "If it turns out the financial future of the shop isn't so dire after all, and both of us can stay on after the new year, we form a truce."

He pushes off the column, stalking my way until he picks up one of my favorite Regency Era historical romances from the table. His fingers drum across the winter-themed cover, then slip it open to reveal the step-back—a scantily dressed couple surrounded by snow, wrapped in an epic clinch.

I stare at them, the shirtless man gazing down at the woman he holds with unbridled longing, his muscular arm clutching her waist; the woman, leaning in, so pliant, eyes hazy, mouth parted. They're a four-and-a-quarter-by-almost-seven-inch ode to sensuality.

"A truce?" I whisper.

Jonathan nods, letting the book cover drop shut. "We co-manage...civilly."

I snort a laugh. My laughter fades as I realize he looks dead serious. "You think that's honestly possible?"

"Financially? Not if things stay as they are, but there's still time for that to change. Interpersonally?" He fans open the book, this time deep into the story. I wrap my hand around his and snap it shut before he cracks the spine. "That remains to be seen."

He peers down, where my hand clasps his, then back up, a flash of something I can't read in those cunning pale eyes beneath thick, dark lashes. "I thought personal-space time was over," he says.

I wrench the book out of his hand. "It was. Until you were about to damage merchandise."

"I was going to buy it."

"The hell you were. It's a romance."

He arches an eyebrow. "Ah, of course. You know everything about me, including all my literary preferences. I don't read romance. I couldn't possibly."

*Shit. Does he?*

I glare at Jonathan as he turns back to the table and once again slides his thrillers toward the front, hating him for making me doubt myself. "Let me guess," I tell him, popping a hip and giving him a skeptical once-over. "Your 'romance reading' consists of *Pride and Prejudice*, and you think Jane Austen was one of the earliest and most influential romance novelists."

He falters for a second, nearly dropping a book as he straightens his thriller stacks into neat tiny towers. "I know there's more to the genre than that," he mutters.

"Hm." I glance down at the historical romance he was allegedly going to buy that I'm now holding. "Maybe you do. This, Mr. Frost, is at least a proper romance novel. In fact, it's my all-time favorite."

In uncharacteristic clumsiness, Jonathan fumbles the stack of thrillers and sends them careening to the floor. His gaze snaps my way, then to the book in my grasp.

"That's *your* favorite?" he says, voice low and tight, pale eyes boring into me.

"Yes," I say, stretching out the word. "Why are you being weird?"

He blinks away, then stares at the shelves full of historical romances. "What are some others? Your favorites."

It's a command. Not a question.

I have no idea why he's acting like this or why I'm about to humor him, but the romance lover in me can't stop herself. I cross the space and stroll across the built in shelves containing historical romances, tapping titles like Vanna White on *Wheel of Fortune*. "This one. This one. This one. This one." I slide my fingertip sensually along the shelf. Jonathan's swallow echoes from ten feet behind me. "This one, too."

I glance over my shoulder. The way Jonathan's staring at me is...terrifying.

I'm the gazelle, and he's the lion. He's unnaturally still, unblinking. And it's freakishly reminiscent of Fantasy Aristocrat Jonathan who walked in, rocking the hell out of breeches and Hessian boots, then shut the library door behind him with an irrevocable, world-changing *click*.

Is nothing safe from him? Must he shoulder and trample his way into every corner of my life? I stand, frozen, unnervingly arrested by the intensity of his gaze, the way he's looking at me like he's seen me right down the marrow of my bones.

I feel naked.

"Are you done messing with me now?" I whisper.

As if my words have broken a spell, he blinks, and then, like a big cat stalking through the grass, he closes the distance between us. "That's what you think I'm doing. Messing with you," he says quietly, eyes searching mine, a new, furious fire in his gaze. "Could you think *any* less of me?"

My chin lifts. Every moment he's snapped and condescended, arrogantly corrected me and put me in my place, flashes through my memory. "Why the *hell* would I think any better?"

Jonathan wraps his hand around mine as I hold the romance novel, staring me down. "You're not entirely wrong," he admits. "I can be cold and calculating, sometimes sharp and abrupt. But this is the truth, whether you believe me or not: I care about the Baileys, this bookshop...*everything* it's given me."

Jonathan plucks the book from my hand, turns, and stalks away. "Even if," I hear him mutter to himself, "it's going to make me lose my goddamn mind."

# CHAPTER 5

Today did not, in fact, turn out to be better. I'm not holding out much hope for tonight, either. After a tense eight hours spent working alongside Jonathan, busting my ass to sell as many books as possible, I come home to an empty apartment. Eli has evening appointments, and June's on night shift at the hospital.

I toast a piece of sourdough, slather it in butter, and inhale every bite along with the bowl of tomato soup that I've heated up, acid reflux be damned.

After that, it's my shower, T-shirt hair wrap, and pajamas routine. Gingerbread happily settled on my lap, I check my computer. My heart does a giddy snow angel when I see there's a message from Mr. Reddit:

> Hey, MCAT. Sorry I was MIA last night. I had a rough day
> at work and decided to cool off with some exercise. It ran
> later than I'd planned, then I came home and crashed.

I make a sympathetic noise and type,

I'm sorry work was rough. But no worries about not messaging—work was shitty for me, too, so I came home, zoned out with a Christmas movie, then went to bed.

*Where you had an elaborate sex dream about an aristocratic Jonathan Frost, the devil on my shoulder whispers. A very long, lurid sex dream.*

The angel on my other side *tut*s disapprovingly.

Sorry to hear that, he types. Does work get more stressful around the holidays? If I remember correctly, it's a busy time of year for you.

My belly swoops. He remembered. It is. I love this time of year, so it's fun but also exhausting. Once it's December, I come home at night and pretty much collapse until we close for the holidays.

And after we close for the holidays this year, I'll have outsold Jonathan Frost and claimed the bookstore for myself again. Glorious victory will be mine!

I let out a villainous cackle and do a spin on my bouncy chair that sends Gingerbread leaping off on a disgruntled meow. When I hear the speakers chime with a new message, I stop my rotations and face the screen.

Don't go too hard, all right? I want you around for the long run. Can't talk shit on Willoughby all by myself.

My heart swan dives off a snow bank and lands in a pillow of powdery glee. I smile so hard, my cheeks hurt. And then I impulsively type something so fucking horrifying, I screech as soon as I hit send: Maybe some time we could meet up and talk shit on Willoughby in person.

"No. NO!" I'm about to click delete to unsend the message, but the read receipt pops up. Oh God. He's seen it. I screech again and slide off my chair to the floor, flailing as I yell, "Why? WHY did I just do that?"

It's this hellacious day's fault. First the naughty dream, then Jonathan bringing me hot cocoa that weirdly wasn't poisoned, the dire bookshop business news, our intense showdown after the Baileys left. My wires are crossed. I've finally cracked.

The speaker chimes again with a new message. Scrambling up from the floor, I read what he wrote: You really want to meet in person? You're not just saying that out of some sad obligation to the guy who's messaged you every night since you met online?

Damn good question, Mr. Reddit. Do I want to meet him? Yes. But I'm also terrified to meet him. Because then he'll know all of me. And he could decide that's not enough or that it's way too much.

But I'll never know if I don't take the risk, will I? What are we going to do, Telegram chat for the next sixty years and never leave the friend zone?

Straightening on my bouncy ball chair, I yank myself closer to the desk and take a deep breath for courage. My hands are shaking as I type. I want to meet you. And I don't feel obligated. Do you?

It says he's typing. I bite my lip so hard, it bleeds.

MCAT. Not to freak you out, but I've wanted to meet you for months. Obligated is the last word I'd use. I just didn't want to come off as a creep.

I blink at the screen, stunned. Mr. Reddit, What_The_Charles_Dickens, has wanted to meet me for months.

Is he...into me? Is this meeting as friends? Potential romantic partners? Friends with potential for romance?

I squint at the screen, repeating the words, examining them. I can't tell. This is why I need Eli and June. They used to tease me about it in college when we were new friends and navigating the dating scene, but they've since learned

I'm truly clueless when someone is romantically interested in me. Maybe it's because attraction doesn't work that way for me or maybe it's because I don't easily perceive people's intent and social cues. If someone smiles warmly and talks to me, I assume they're friendly and have something they think I'll enjoy talking with them about. That's it. June and Eli have to clue me in when someone's putting on the moves.

I'd give anything for their insight right now, but neither of them are here, and even if they were, I'm not sure I'd be ready to confess how invested I am in Mr. Reddit and meeting him in person.

It's moments like this that I wish I'd met him yesterday. Months ago. And I'm about to propose we rip off the Band Aid and meet ASAP...but then I think about what a risk meeting up will be. It could be great. It could be disastrous. And if it's a disaster, I'm going to be crushed.

I can't chance that right now. Not with what's going on at work. I need to put all my energy into kickass sales, securing my job, and saving Bailey's Bookshop.

With a big mopey frown on my face, I type, So, please believe me. I really do want to meet, and I wish we could meet soon, but I think it'll be best to wait until I'm on holiday break. Is that okay?

Of course, he writes. It's best for me as well.

Work intense for you, too? I type.

It's...complex. It's a bit of an uphill battle right now. I work for people who I think the world of but who are deeply resistant to a plan I've drawn up to fully modernize their sales approach. I've spent nearly a year building this out. I have a solid rationale and the numbers to back it up. It will save their business. But they're wary of it.

I'm a little surprised he's been so forthcoming about work, since we don't generally share personal details, but I'm not complaining. It's...sort of lovely, hearing more about him, learning how he's navigating this professional challenge.

Technophobic traditionalists? I venture, smiling as I think of the Baileys.

Unfortunately, he writes back. I know why they want to keep things the way they are, what they're afraid of losing if they embrace my idea, but they're going to fold in the first quarter, otherwise. They don't stand a chance without this.

I sigh sadly, thinking of the bookshop and Mrs. Bailey's warning that we might not open our doors after New Year's. Do you think they'll listen?

I hope so. Not just because it's sound business, but because I care about the people there and what they believe in. They're very different from me, all heart and nostalgia and being a part of the neighborhood. When I started off working on this plan, I saw it as a business challenge, a puzzle to solve. But somewhere along the way, it changed—I wanted to fight to save the place for them, because they mattered to me. And then I realized I'd started fighting to save it for me, because it mattered to me, too.

My heart squeezes. I type, It sounds like you really love them—where you work and who you work with.

You see it that way? his response chimes immediately. As love?

I do. Just because you're loving them differently than they love doesn't make it any less loving. My mom says there are countless kinds of love, and love enough for everyone. That love is an infinite resource whose expressions are just as innumerable.

He doesn't respond for a minute. Then, Very few people would recognize how I operate as love.

Thus, I type, your deep connection with Fitzwilliam Darcy.

LOL. Except without the "wet shirt after diving in the lake" to redeem me.

I laugh. That's only in the movie anyway! Darcy's more than

lovable as he is in the book, at least by the end, and that's the point of a good character arc—he grows. He learns to admit his mistakes, as does Lizzie. Two people, who couldn't have hated each other more at the outset while battling inconvenient desire, ultimately choose humility and forgiveness.

Beautifully said, he writes. It's like you love Austen or something, MCAT.

I smile, self-consciousness heating my cheeks. I mean, she's the quintessential voice of romance.

Am I ever going to live that down?!

I'm just teasing you. Merciless teasing has become a reflex for me. A skill I've developed at my job.

Sounds like a highly professional environment, he writes. What are your coworkers like?

I only have one. And he's just as bad as me.

How so? he writes.

I hesitate, because generally we keep away from personal specifics, but he opened up about his work, and this tension with Jonathan is painfully bottled up inside me. Even if I twist the cork just a little, release the tiniest bit of pressure, I think I'll feel better. We're not friendly the rest of the year, but December is our worst month. He can't stand the holidays. I adore them. It takes our antagonism to a whole new level.

There's no response for a minute. Then he finally writes, Have I ruined my chances if I admit I'm not very festive myself?

I breathe out slowly, weathering my first disappointment as the daydreams that I've indulged—Mr. Reddit and me window shopping, admiring the Winter Wonderland show at the conservatory as snow falls around us, skating at the downtown rink, hand in hand—dissolve. But he has every right not to be festive. Like Eli said, for some people, the holidays just don't feel celebratory, and that's valid.

*He said that so you'd consider showing Jonathan some compassion, the angel on my shoulder reminds me. How's that going for you?*

The devil on my other side reaches for the extendable handle of her pitchfork while the angel's wings pop out this time, prepared for an attack and ready for flight.

*Have I ruined my chances?* I mull over those words. Do they mean what I think they mean?

I force myself to be brave and type, Of course not. Though, what kind of "chances" are you talking about?

There's a pause for a moment, then he's typing.

I want to be your friend, MCAT, not just online but in person —that goes without saying. And when I talk to you, all I can think is I want a hell of a lot more, too, but I've tried to stop myself from going there. There are a hundred things you might not like about me in real life. I haven't wanted to get my hopes up. I'm still afraid to.

I've been thinking that way, too, I admit, relieved that he's felt how I have. Worried you won't like me once you see how different the real me can be from the online version.

The chat's silent, no typing alerts, no cheery chimes. He's thinking. We both are.

So...this might sound extreme, he types, maybe a bit harsh, but hear me out—what if we stop talking until we meet? Give ourselves some time to reset our expectations, to separate the people we've been behind these screens from the people we'll meet in real life?

My stomach drops. I think about how much I'll miss talking to him, how empty my evenings will feel. But, as I mull it over, what he says makes a lot of sense. If we take time away from each other, it'll be a fresh start. A chance to meet each other with a blank slate. And I can use this time to focus solely on work and kicking Jonathan Frost's ass at sales. As much as it bums me out, I think Mr. Reddit's on to something.

I think that's smart, I type. Pulling Gingerbread tight into my arms to console myself, I earn her sleepy, half-awake meow. It'll be weird not talking.

It will, he writes. I'll miss it.

Me, too. But it'll be worth it in the end. Like Marianne's heartbreak.

SPOILERS, CATWOOD!

I snort a laugh, happy for a reason to smile rather than feel sad.

Another message from him pops up on a chime. I'll message soon with some ideas about where to meet and when, and you can tell me what sounds good. Does that work?

That's perfect, I type.

Good. Take care of yourself, MCAT. And sleep well.

Spoiler alert: I don't sleep well at all.

# CHAPTER 6

### PLAYLIST: "WINTER WONDERLAND," SHE & HIM

I feel like the walking dead. I've barely slept in a week. Because every night, I'm scared to pick up a romance novel—audio or otherwise—to read myself to sleep and risk another erotic aristocrat dream starring Jonathan Frost. And then I lay in bed, staring at the ceiling for hours, because when I deviate from my bedtime routine, my sleep is shit.

Too bad. I can't cave. No romance novels by night, no salacious duke and bluestocking fantasies starring Jonathan Frost and yours truly. Not only because I don't *want* to fantasize about Jonathan Frost, but because it's not smart to, either, when I'm doing everything I can to take that sucker down as well as counting down the days until I meet Mr. Reddit, the man who *used* to star in my dreams, until Jonathan Jerkface Frost shouldered his way in like a pushy, decadently sexual, cunnilingus-obsessed lover who—

*Stop it, brain! Stop!*

I'm losing it. I'm sleep-deprived and suffering, missing Mr. Reddit, and furious with Mr. Frost. I've spent the first week of our bargain busting my butt at work while running on fumes, and I don't even have the most sales to show for it.

Jonathan was right, that thriller flew off the shelves. And not just that title—he's been selling all kinds of slashers like hotcakes. So much for holiday cheer. Who buys violent novels portraying the worst human impulses in the time of year dedicated to peace on earth and goodwill toward all?

I can't dwell on it or I get *really* angry.

I have to focus on the positive. Yes, I'm behind on sleep and on sales, and no, I did not see such an ass-whooping coming this past week, but this suffering won't last forever. One exhausting week down, only two more to go. And today I have Eli, who's going to get me back on track with my sales.

"Have I told you you're a lifesaver, Elijah?"

"A time or twenty," he says, shouldering open the coffee shop door and holding it for me. We shiver as we step outside, clutching our hot to-go cups against the frigid outside air. "And I'm inclined to agree with you, considering I already came in and read Hanukkah books just a few weeks ago. Speaking of, you've been thin on the details about story time today. What's the plan?"

I sip my hot cocoa and avoid his eyes. "Oh, a little bit of this. A little bit of that..."

Eli slows to a stop on the sidewalk. "Gabriella Sofia Di Natale, what have you done?"

"I might have advertised that our guest reader is a well-loved local child therapist, and that his book, *Color My Feelings*, was a featured title today in the bookstore, and that perhaps, possibly, he'd sign purchased copies, and sugar cookies are involved—don't worry I have baby wipes, but that's why I made you bring a change of clothes, just in case—I'm sorry, I know I'm the worst friend ever." I gasp for air after spewing that in one long guilt-soaked exhale.

Eli stares at me. "You're foisting on me not only sugared-up children, but parents who think I'm a walking free therapeutic consult *on my day off.*"

"I promise Jonathan will kick out anyone who's a jerk. After I make them apologize and buy three copies of your book. Zero tolerance for assholery."

Eli glares at me.

I stick out my bottom lip and give him big sad puppy eyes. "I'm sorry, okay? I'm desperate."

Sighing, he hooks arms with me and resumes our walk down the sidewalk. "I forgive you, but *only* if you return the favor."

"Anything," I tell him, foolishly.

He smiles at me, batting long auburn eyelashes, "Come with me to Luke's hockey game tonight."

"Tonight?" I whine. "It'll be so late. And so cold."

"You love the cold."

"I love the *snow*," I correct him.

Eli lifts an eyebrow. "Did you forget the part where you sold me out to boost your sales, then promised to make it up to me?"

"Uh. Maybe?"

"Gabby. I need moral support. Luke's been so bummed that I can never make any of his games, but I've been secretly relieved work gets in the way, because I don't know *anything* about hockey. I need you to teach me the basics so I don't make an ass of myself."

"El, he doesn't expect you to do a post-game breakdown."

"I know, but I want him to feel like he can talk to me about it and I'll understand why it was a good game or it wasn't, why he played well or struggled. I *want* to get it."

I wiggle my eyebrows as we stop outside the bookshop. "Wow. This is serious. Elijah Goldberg wants to learn a *sport* for his boyfriend."

"Exactly," he says, opening the door, then gently shoving me past it. "So come with me tonight and you're forgiven for everything I'm about to endure. I'll drive. You'll DJ a sick holiday playlist for the ride. I'll buy you hot cocoa with extra marshmallows. You'll explain the game to me. It's a plan."

"If I can stay awake through the game," I grumble.

"Like that would matter," he says. "You could explain it in your sleep."

"You try having a dad who's in the Hockey Hall of Fame and see if you come out unscathed. I mutter Stanley Cup stats when I'm in REM. Do you understand how disturbing that is?"

"Woah—" Eli wraps his hand around my arm, bringing us to a stop. "Is that him?"

I glance toward the back of the store, where Jonathan stands, facing away and restocking a fresh batch of mysteries he sold out of yesterday. Except this time, he's placing them on the shelves right at eye level.

"That motherfucker," I hiss, storming toward him and dragging Eli with me. "He moved my small-town Alaskan romance!"

"So that *is* him," Eli whispers. "Holy shit, Gabby."

"Shut up. Don't even say it."

"He's so hot."

I throw Eli a death glare. "What would Luke say?"

"Luke would say I have eyeballs. I said he's hot, not that I want to bang him."

"Good. Because I'll be doing the banging—of his head into a wall," I mutter.

Hearing us, Jonathan glances over his shoulder, eyes narrowing at Eli before they snap back my way. "Miss Di Natale."

"You moved my romances."

He arches a dark eyebrow. "It's fine. I'll introduce myself." Extending a hand toward Eli, he says, "Jonathan Frost."

"Elijah Goldberg." Eli smiles up at Jonathan, a definite

63

twinkle in his eye. I step on his toe, making him wince. "Damn, Gabby."

"Ah, so she's this angelic with everyone," Jonathan says.

Eli laughs. I scowl. Jonathan smirks. If I had magical powers, I'd send the garland-strewn candelabra overhead crashing down on him.

"So, Gabriella," Jonathan says, "I didn't know this was Bring Your *Friend* to Work Day."

"It isn't. It's Bring Your Roommate-the-pediatric-therapist-and-published-children's-author-for-a-story-time-and-marathon-book-signing Day," I tell him on a wide, triumphant smile.

"Roommate," Jonathan repeats. His jaw does that aggravated ticking thing. He's white-knuckling the mysteries he clutches in both hands.

Eli wraps an arm around my waist and smiles over at me. "We're best friends, too. Since she was a lowly freshman who made a pass at my fine senior ass."

"Did not! Saying I couldn't find the library was *not* a pickup line!"

Eli grins. "I like my version better." He turns back to Jonathan. "I showed her where the library was, we hit it off, and since her sophomore year, we've lived together."

Jonathan blinks. "Lived together. You. Her."

"With June, too," Eli says blithely, "who was two years below me, one above Gabby. June and I had a pre-rec together, then June hit it off with Gabby when I introduced them while we were studying at the library. I'm the glue who made the three of us roommates, when they were still in undergrad and I stuck around for my master's."

Something shifts in Jonathan's expression. "Ah. I see."

Eli tips his head. "This probably sounds weird, but...you look familiar."

Jonathan stares at him for a minute. "Yeah, come to think of it, you do, too."

"No kids, right?"

"God, no," Jonathan says. "Not yet, at least."

I try and fail utterly to picture Jonathan possessing a single affectionate bone in his body. "You know children need things like warmth and smiles and conversation that exceeds bone-dry sarcasm, right, Frost?"

Jonathan gives me a withering glare.

"Maybe we go to the same gym?" Eli says warmly, trying to smooth things over.

Jonathan glances his way. "Yeah, maybe that's it. I'm a member at the place down on..."

Leaving those two to their irritating little bonding session, I extract myself from Eli's grip and head for the break room to hang up my coat. Their conversation continues without me, and by the time I come back, they look thick as thieves, unwrapping the holiday cookie plates that I ordered for story time since I was too exhausted to bake, bonding over sugar's detrimental effect on the body.

I clear my throat loudly. Their eyes meet mine.

Tapping my wristwatch, I arch one eyebrow, a perfect imitation of Jonathan. His mouth quirks at the corner before he covers it with his hand and clears his throat. "It's like looking in a mirror," he says.

I stick out my tongue.

"Now that I don't do."

Ignoring Jonathan, I turn toward my former-best-friend-turned-traitor and tell him, "Thirty minutes until showtime, Elijah."

My phone starts buzzing in my dress pocket as Eli and Jonathan go back to chitchatting. In fact, I realize belatedly it's been buzzing for a while. Extracting it, I feel my shoulders lift toward my neck. Another message from a number I don't recognize. But I know who it is.

*Did you get the flowers?*

*I want to talk.*

*Please, Gabby. It's been six months. Can't you give me another chance?*

"What is it?" Eli says, watching me white-knuckle my phone.

I shake my head, blocking the number, then slipping my phone back into my dress. "Nothing. Now you'll excuse me. I need a word with Mr. Frost."

Marching past Jonathan, I flick a finger toward the back room. Jonathan grumbles something under his breath, then follows me.

When I reach the archway leading to the kitchenette, I stop and spin, facing him. His eyes snap up from my ass. He has the grace to look a little abashed, and there's a blush darkening his cheeks.

"You done?" I ask.

His eyes dart away. "I didn't mean—" He clears his throat, tugging at his collar. "You have tinsel on your..."

"Ah." I feel behind me and there it is, a nice strip of silver tinsel clinging to my butt. I yank it off and clear my throat, too. "Right. Well. Back to business. I need your help with story time and the book signing afterward."

He arches an eyebrow and leans a shoulder against the archway, arms across his chest. "*My* help for an event that's going to disproportionately boost *your* sales." He clucks his tongue. "No dice, Di Natale."

"Jonathan." I step closer, lowering my voice. "Please. I need someone to keep the mob in check. Parents can be entitled shitheads."

He leans in and says, "I know. Which is why I don't bother with them."

A growl rolls out of me. "I promised Eli you'd make sure anyone who's out of line gets the boot."

"And that's my fault?" Jonathan glances down and extracts his phone from his pocket as it makes a repeated ding.

"Jonathan, can't that wait?"

"You're quite the hypocrite, Gabriella, given you just checked *your* phone a moment ago." He frowns at his screen, wiping his forehead with his free hand. I notice his face is damp, like he's sweating. His hand is shaking a little.

For just a moment, my empathy wins out over my annoyance. "Are you okay?"

"Fine," he snaps, pocketing his phone, then strolling past me toward his coat hook.

I gape as I spin and follow his path. "We were in the middle of a conversation."

"Conversation's over." He unhooks his messenger bag, which holds the laptop he's always tapping on whenever customers aren't around. It has a screen shield so I can't see shit. Trust me, I've tried. Bag on his shoulder, he storms into the bookkeeping room and shuts the door behind him with a *thud.*

Stunned, I clench my teeth and stare up at the ceiling. Irony of ironies, we were standing under mistletoe.

"Gabriella!" Eli calls.

"What?" I hustle back to the main room and the sight of Eli, snowflake-shaped cookie in hand, seated in the wingback chair I positioned right by the gas fireplace, a giant pile of *Color Your Feelings* beside him.

"Sweet Lord," he says, equal parts horror and reverence as he takes in how many copies await his signature. "That's a lot."

Smiling, I offer him a handful of thin black Sharpies. "Get ready to autograph, Mr. Goldberg."

He glances out the storefront window at the growing line

outside and mutters, "I hope they go into triple overtime tonight."

"Knowing my luck, Eli, they will."

Despite my grumbling about this late-night hockey game, I can't help but smile as we enter and get our first glimpse of the rink. I love the atmosphere—the scrape and *shoosh* of blades on ice, the cold, dry air filling my lungs.

A wave of happiness washes over me as I lift my phone, snap a photo, then send it to my parents.

**ME:** Why does every hockey rink have that same magical feel?

My phone buzzes immediately.

**MOM:** The feeling of freezing your ass off while breathing in the smell of sweaty bodies and ripe hockey gear?

**DAD:** You mean the feeling of being pleasantly chilled while admiring gorgeous specimens of perspiring athletic glory?

**DAD:** Your mother just snorted at that. I'm offended.

**MOM:** I'll make it up to you later.

I shudder. They're 100 percent sitting on opposite ends of the couch, playing footsie while they do this.

**ME:** Stop flirting in the family text. It's gross.

**MOM:** I'm done, promise.

**DAD:** Who's playing, kiddo?

**ME:** Eli's boyfriend. He's in the local competitive league.

**DAD:** Those guys are pretty skilled. Should be fun to watch. What made you want to go?

**ME:** Eli. He did me a solid for work so I'm returning the favor with a hockey tutorial.

Eli takes me by the elbow when we start to ascend the stands, while I focus on wrapping up with my parents. Just as he guides us to our seats, I pocket my phone. "Sorry, got caught in the family chat."

"You're fine." Sitting beside me, he scours the rink and smiles when he spots Luke. His smile becomes a grimace when Luke checks a guy into the boards. "I can't believe your dad did this. He's the biggest teddy bear, and hockey is such a..."

"Brutal game?" I shrug. "Yeah, it is."

My dad, Nicholas Sokolov, is one of the greatest forwards to ever play the game. On the rink, he was always pure, fiery hunger; but off, he is and always has been the gentlest person I know. When I first started watching him play, it was a shock to see that scrappy man out on the ice.

Eli's gaze tracks Luke as he says, "I suppose I shouldn't be surprised. Luke's a teddy bear, too, and look at him." Luke throws his shoulder into the other team's offense and wins the puck, then skates toward the bench.

"Wait, why is Luke leaving already?" Eli asks.

"His shift is over."

"He was on the ice for sixty seconds!"

"Less than that. More like forty-five. It doesn't sound like a long time, but it's tough. Hockey's an anaerobic sport—you go as hard as you can the whole time you're on the ice, switch, catch your breath, hydrate, then go back out there."

"So he's not being penalized," Eli says.

"Nope. He's doing exactly what he's supposed to."

Eli beams. "Good."

Answering more of Eli's questions, I explain icing and offsides and why some hits are deemed fair and others aren't. As the players switch again, I notice the tallest guy of the bunch swing his long legs over the boards, then shoot across the ice like he was born to be there. A *zing* of awareness bolts down my spine. Goosebumps dance over my skin.

There's something familiar about him.

"That guy's fast," Eli says. "Number 12."

I nod dazedly, trying to ignore my pounding heart as I tug back on my headphones. I can feel a goal coming, and soon the horn announcing it will blare at a volume my brain can't handle.

My eyes track Number 12, riveted, curiosity clawing at me. Who *is* he?

It's difficult to get a sense of a player's body when they're in their pads and gear, but there's something so familiar about the breadth of his shoulders, the long line of his legs, a lick of dark hair curling up at the bottom of his helmet.

I stare at him as if simply looking long enough will solve the riddle. I know him. I swear I do.

For the next thirty seconds, Number 12 is all I think about, all I see, lithe and lightning-fast on the ice, leading his side's offensive momentum, backtracking when his teammate loses the puck and the other team's defense sends it to their forwards. He's there in a flash, gaining possession, exploding in a fresh burst of speed across the ice. Bearing down on the goalie, he fakes a slapshot, cuts past the crease, then cheekily backhands it into the net, right over the goalie's shoulder.

The light blazes red, and my headphones dull the roaring blare of the horn to a faint hum. Eli cheers, smiling as he pats my thigh in his excitement.

Number 12 isn't a hot-dogger. He simply lifts his chin to acknowledge his teammates who swarm him. I don't see his smile behind that mouthguard, if he smiles at all. The crush of players block my view, slapping his helmet and hugging him.

But I do see his eyes. Because they drift right up the stands and land on me.

Wintergreen. Arctic cold.

I gasp.

"What?" Eli says, turning toward me. "What is it?"

Holy shit. Number 12 is Jonathan Frost.

# CHAPTER 7

## PLAYLIST: "SANTA BABY," HALEY REINHART

"I have to go," I shoot up from my seat.

"Don't be ridiculous. I drove you." Eli clasps my hand and tugs me back down. I land with a flop. "What's going on?"

"Th-th-that's—" I gesticulate wildly toward the ice, where Jonathan's still staring up at me, a familiar frustrated notch in his brow that I can feel even from this distance. "That's Jonathan."

"Jonathan who—*ohhhhh*." Eli glances back toward the ice and squints. "Wow, it is him! I knew he looked familiar. That must be why. Maybe he's a friend of Lukey's." Eli waves.

I slap his hand down. "Do not wave at him. He's the enemy. Nemesis. Antagonist. Provocateur."

"Okay, Thesaurus.com, relax. You're not at work. Think you can set that aside right now? He's on Luke's team, and we want Luke to win!"

I gape at Eli as he wedges his hot tea between his thighs, then sets two fingers in his mouth and whistles loudly. "Woohoo!"

"This is the worst," I mutter into my hot chocolate.

"Might as well make the best of it," he says. "Because you definitely owe me this whole game."

"Ellllliiiii," I whine.

He glances over at me sharply. "Two hours, Gabriella. I signed books and read stories and held kids with sticky, sugar-cookie fingers on my lap like freaking Santa Claus for *two hours* today."

And Jonathan never showed his face, never helped. He stayed holed up in the bookkeeping room, doing whatever covert shit he does on his laptop, and left me to the whim of my own devices, damn him. Thankfully, the parents were on their best behavior.

"Fair point," I tell Eli. "But if I have to see Jonathan when this game is over, don't ask me to be nice."

Eli rolls his eyes, turning back to the game. "And you call *him* Scrooge."

Begrudgingly, I have to admit the game is fun to watch, just like Dad promised. At least, it's fun, until Jonathan turns into the MVP.

After his first goal, the opposition ties it up right before the first period ends. In the second period, Eli's boyfriend, Luke, who's a defensemen, has an incredible breakaway with Jonathan and an assist for Jonathan's second goal. Then in the third period, the other team ties it up, but with two minutes to spare, Jonathan scores once more, which not only wins the game but makes for a hat trick.

He's going to be insufferable at work tomorrow.

I try hard not to pout like a five-year-old as we wait for Luke after the game, but I'm struggling. Eli drove us, so I'm stuck until he's ready to go—a plan I was fine with before I knew I'd be bumping into Jonathan Frost.

I really don't know if I can take seeing him like this, after kicking ass at my favorite sport, sweaty and showered and glowing with pride, high on adrenaline and arrogant as hell.

In fact, I know I can't.

The first of the players exits their locker room, and my heart springboards from my chest to my throat. Spinning, I start for the lobby doors. "I'm going to wait in the car."

"You'll need my keys," Eli says, a little too pleased with himself. "Seeing as it's locked."

I freeze, pivot, then freeze again. Shit. I'm too late.

Because strolling out of the locker room, shoulder to shoulder with Luke, is Jonathan. His dark hair's wet and wavier than normal, a thick lock out of its normal tidy order brushing his forehead. He glances up and air whooshes out of my lungs. His cheeks are pink from exertion, and there's a fiery glint in his pale green eyes.

My legs wobble a little.

Eli grabs my elbow. "You okay?"

"Uh."

"A certain someone isn't making you weak at the knees, is he?" Eli says out of the side of his mouth. I elbow him so hard, he wheezes, "You need anger management classes."

"I know. It's his fault." So many things are Jonathan's fault. The relentless heartburn I've developed in the past year, the ache in my knuckles from my hands forming fists all day, the deplorable dream that's sabotaged my sleep. And now, he's responsible for every drop of liquid heat flooding my veins, pooling low and aching-sweet between my legs.

It's as if my libido—sometimes extinguished, other times a faint, quiet flame coaxed to life in the air of connection—is now a consuming wildfire, devouring every moment we're together, burning hotter and brighter. I can't stand it.

Clearing my throat, I try to look dignified as I meet his eyes. "Jonathan."

"Gabriella." His mouth tips up at the corner, a satisfied near-grin that makes my stomach flip-flop. "An unexpected surprise. This is a little much, though, don't you think—following me to my game? If you wanted to see me outside of work, a simple text would have sufficed."

"Ha-ha." I set a hand on my stomach and tell it to stop doing backflips as I jerk my head toward Eli giving Luke a congratulatory kiss. "I was brought here against my will."

Jonathan's gaze dances over me. "Like what you saw?"

I roll my eyes. "You know your performance was impressive."

His eyebrows lift. A blush blooms on his already flushed cheeks. "Wow."

"Don't—" I point a finger at him. "I didn't mean it like that."

He lifts both hands innocently. "I just said 'wow.'"

"I'm so glad you came," Luke tells Eli.

"Me too." Eli smiles up at him. "You were amazing."

"Not as amazing as this guy," Luke says, shoving Jonathan's shoulder playfully. Jonathan doesn't budge. "He stepped it up tonight. Putting on a show for someone, big guy?"

For the first time, I see someone else earn that arctic glare. "I played like I always play."

"Uh-huh." Turning my way, Luke offers me a fist to pound. "Gabby. Thanks for coming."

I glance away from Jonathan and smile up at Luke, who is absurdly good looking. Dark skin, amber eyes, the kind of bone structure that June covets and recreates with her daily contouring makeup routine. "You did good, kid," I tell him.

Luke flashes me a wide, bright smile. "Well, coming from you, that's something."

"What's that mean?" Jonathan says, glancing between us.

"Nothing." I give Luke a look. I don't throw around who my dad is. People are fanatical about him. It's a big part of why I go by my mom's maiden name. Sokolov is a fairly common Russian last name, but in the States, and especially this hockey-obsessed town where Dad spent the last five years of his career before retiring, people immediately associate "Sokolov" with him.

Luke mouths *sorry*, then turns to Jonathan. "I forgot to make introductions. My bad! Gabby, this is my good friend, Jonny. Jonny, this is Gabby. She's—"

"I know Gabriella," Jonathan says, and there's an odd edge to his voice. "What I *didn't* know was that Eli, your boyfriend, is Elijah, her roommate."

"Or that Luke's friend, Jonny," Eli says, "is Jonathan, her coworker." The four of us glance between each other.

"Wow," Luke says. "This is weird. So, wait—oh *shit*." His eyes widen as he looks from me to Jonathan. "So she's—"

Luke doesn't get to finish that sentence because Jonathan drops his gear bag, hockey stick and all, right on Luke's foot, making him swear foully just as a group of kids walks by.

"Come on, man," a player from their team calls, hands over both sides of his kid's head. "Little ears."

"Sorry," Luke mutters their way, hopping on one foot before he says to Jonathan, "What the hell?"

Jonathan bends over, hikes up his gear bag again, then says without any remorse, "Oops."

Luke glares at Jonathan. Jonathan glares at Luke. Another neurotypical eye conversation flies right over my head.

"Well," Eli says, smiling brightly at everyone. "What a small world!"

Glancing away from Jonathan, Luke says to us, "Ready to grab some food?"

I deflate. It's ten at night, and even with my day off yesterday, after a week of shit sleep, I'm deliriously tired. I don't want to go out to eat. I want to go to bed. But I know Eli's dying to be with Luke. They're both busy professionals and don't see each other nearly as much as they'd like. He's been counting on this time.

"I'm wiped," I admit. "Maybe you could drop me off at home on your way?"

Eli bites his lip. "Luke wanted to hit the diner right down the road here."

"They have the best grilled cheese," Luke says. "Oh, and milkshakes. Just the thing for your sweet tooth."

"Gabriella doesn't like milkshakes," Jonathan tells him, eyes on me. "Just peppermint chocolate milk."

"Peppermint *hot cocoa*," I remind him.

"Semantics," Jonathan says, coming damn close to a proper smile. "It's definitely not milkshakes."

It's familiar territory, going back and forth like this, except there's none of the usual bite in our words. It feels lived in, almost...friendly.

"I hate to say it," I tell Luke and Eli, though my eyes oddly refuse to leave Jonathan. "He's right. I don't like milkshakes. The texture is not my thing. But I can still hang in there and come—"

"I'll take you home," Jonathan says.

Luke hesitates then asks, "You sure?"

Eli glances between us. "We don't want to inconvenience anyone—"

"It's fine," I announce, my eyes locked with Jonathan's.

This is fine. It's no big deal. In fact, it's an excellent opportunity to prove that this raging libido nonsense is just that—nonsense. I'm going to ride in Jonathan Frost's car for thirty minutes back to the city, not melt into a horny puddle, and show us both how cool as a cucumber *I* can be.

"There you have it," Jonathan tells them. He sets a hand low on my back, guiding me in front of him. I suck in a breath because, holy *shit*, does that feel good—the heat of his touch seeping through my coat. I lean into it just a little, like a cat curling up to an affectionate hand. This is not boding well for the cool-as-a-cucumber plan.

We're hurtling past Luke and Eli.

"Uh, bye?" I glance over my shoulder and see the two of them, all smiles, looking annoyingly pleased. "They're such menaces," I mutter.

"Tell me about it." Reaching past me and opening the lobby door for us, Jonathan points his fob at a sturdy, unpretentious black SUV that beeps twice obediently as he unlocks it.

When I get closer, I realize it's not one of those low crossover cars masquerading as an SUV. It's a proper truck chassis, high up and formidable. "Yeesh, it's big." As soon as it's out of my mouth, I realize how that sounds. I glance at Jonathan. "I swear I did not mean for that to come out like innuendo."

"Never even considered it." Except Jonathan's almost smiling again, eyes down on the ground as he clears his throat.

Then he opens my door and offers me a hand. I stare at it in confusion. He doesn't like that.

"Christ, Gabby. I didn't spit on my palm. It's just a hand up."

I've never heard him say my name, not the name everyone else uses. I'm not sure how I feel about the fact that my skin's humming and my cheeks are warm, and the sound of my name on his lips echoes in the snowy silence. *Gabby*.

Our eyes hold.

My fingertips inch closer to his outstretched hand.

I don't know why I'm doing it. I don't know how to stop.

"Why?" I ask softly.

Snow drifts from the sky, dusting Jonathan's dark hair and his midnight-black windbreaker. His throat works in a swallow, then he says, "Because I want to."

It's hardly an answer, but apparently it's answer enough for me. Because somehow I find my fingertips brushing his, sliding over calluses and rough skin, until our palms connect.

Air seeps from my lungs. His grip is warm and solid as he leverages me up, and just when I'm telling myself that no, this isn't some Darcy-hoists-Elizabeth-into-her-carriage-and-the-world-tips-on-its-axis moment, his thumb brushes the back of my hand. Apparently there's a nerve expressway between that spot and every erogenous zone in my body, because I drop like a rag doll onto my seat, a drumbeat of longing thudding through my limbs.

If Jonathan feels anything close to what I just did, he doesn't show it. His face is unreadable, his features smooth as he shuts my door.

*What was that about not melting into a horny puddle?* The little devil on my shoulder cackles as she traces a flame in the air with her pitchfork. *You are so lusting over him.*

The angel on my other side gives the devil a prim, reproachful look. *She's supposed to be lusting after Mr. Reddit.*

Seething, I stare ahead at the swirling snow outside the car. I hate that both angel and devil are right. I hate that I want to be keyed up for Mr. Reddit and instead it's Jonathan Frost who's turned me into a hot, lusty mess while he's as cool and calm as ever.

But as I watch him round the car, his long, broad body wrapped in a swirl of fast-falling snow, his hand flexes, then balls into a brutal fist.

Maybe someone's not so unaffected, after all.

Smug with satisfaction, I wet my thumb and index finger, then pinch out the flame blazing in the air, because if he's lusting as bad as I am, that makes it...neutral. Or something.

The tiny devil on my shoulder scowls. The angel beams in approval.

Jonathan wrenches open his door, then slides in. Frowning, he opens his phone, then taps an app icon I can't see. So I crane my neck a little. "Stop snooping, Gabriella."

I glance away, red-cheeked and embarrassed. "You were practically flashing it my way."

"I was not."

"Was too."

"*Were* too," he corrects.

"Argh!" I throw up my hands, then reach for the door handle. "I'm walking home."

The car doors' locks click. Slowly, I turn and face him. "This is how I die, isn't it?"

Jonathan scrubs his face before his hands drop to his lap. He turns his head and stares at me. "Gabriella."

"Jonathan."

"Please don't threaten to walk home in the snow. Or joke about me killing you." He reaches in the center console and flips open a tiny door, revealing a small stash of...candy?

"Who are you?" I ask as I watch him efficiently unwrap two mini peanut butter cups, then pop them in his mouth.

"Jonathan Frost, co-manager that you love to hate. I thought we covered this." Chewing briskly, he pushes the button to start his car.

"You have *candy* in your vehicle." A shiver wracks me. My teeth start to chatter. "You eat s-sugar? And enjoy it?"

"I'm a man of many mysteries, Gabriella. Help yourself."

I peer toward the console. There's... "M-mint chocolate M&Ms?" My teeth clack so hard, I barely get the words out.

"All yours." He turns on my seat warmer, then cranks up the heat and points all the vents my way.

My belly does a disconcerting swoop. He noticed that I'm cold. He's making sure I'm warm. "You don't like them?"

"Not a bit," he says. "Mint chocolate is foul."

"Then why do you have mint chocolate M&Ms?"

Jonathan drops back in his seat again and rakes a hand

through his hair, tugging hard, jaw working until he finally says, "Because I saw them at the grocery store after work today and thought of you and bought them. Because I was an ass this morning, and I regret that, and I bought apology candy, and then I realized how ridiculous that was, when I'm starting to think there aren't enough M&Ms in the world to make things better between us."

I'm nothing short of stunned by this admission.

There's a thick beat of silence. I stare down at the M&Ms. Jonathan stares out at the snow.

Finally, he breaks the stillness, reaching for a stainless-steel canteen in his cup holder, drinking from it in two long gulps that make his Adam's apple bob and infuriatingly make me think about dragging my tongue up his throat. Then he checks his phone again. After reading whatever it says, he seems satisfied. He throws the car in reverse and starts to back out.

I'm still in shock. "So...you bought these...because of me? Because you felt bad about this morning?"

Jonathan stops the vehicle with a jolt halfway out of the parking space, then turns and faces me. Suddenly this big SUV feels very small. "Is it *that* unbelievable?"

"Uh...Well..." I lick my lips. This feels like a test. One that I'm definitely going to fail.

"It's not," he tells me, because apparently I said that out loud. "And you can't fail it. You just answer the question."

I stare at him curiously, the strong lines of his nose and cheekbones. His striking pale eyes glowing in the faint light. There's this...*pull*, deep inside me, begging me to climb over the console, straddle his lap, and kiss him until I taste bitter-sweet chocolate and winter air, until I breathe in the warmth of his skin, hot and clean from exercise followed by a quick scrub with soap that makes him smell like a long, snowy walk in a forest of evergreens.

And I don't understand that. I don't understand why it feels like something's dragging me, inch by inch, toward Jonathan Frost. It shouldn't be happening. Not when, in just a few weeks, I'll meet the guy I truly care about, and this Mr. Freeze mutant I work with will be out of my life for good.

What is *wrong* with me?

"Hell if I know," I mutter, answering both Jonathan's quandary and mine. Soothing the pain of my existential crisis, I open the mint chocolate M&Ms and dump half the bag down my throat.

Jonathan sighs as he resumes pulling out of the parking space. "So much sugar, Gabriella."

"Hush up, you," I tell him. "You bought them for me. Out of…remorse, which, wow, that sounds weird."

His grip on the steering wheel tightens. His jaw tics, emphasizing the hollow in his cheeks and the promise of a dimple, if he ever smiled. It's shadowed with dark, dense stubble, and just looking at it, I can feel its sandpaper scruff abrading my thighs. My mind runs with that, imagining hot, wet kisses from that stern mouth wetting my skin, trailing higher, higher, until—

"I mean it," Jonathan says, wrenching me from my lusty thoughts. "I'm sorry. I know…I know I get short sometimes and I make abrupt exits." He pauses, as if searching for what to say next. "It has nothing to do with you, but it affects you. And…I'm sorry."

I stare at him, the M&Ms lowering to my lap. It's weird, experiencing an ounce of contrition from Jonathan Frost, hearing him own his less-endearing qualities and apologize for them, but…I believe him. So, shifting slightly in my seat to see him better, I tell him, "I…forgive you."

Eyes on the road, he says, "That sounded painful."

"Saying 'I forgive you'?" I laugh faintly. "It kinda was.

We've been hostile for so long, I don't really know how to speak to you otherwise."

Jonathan's silent, his brow furrowed. He looks worried.

For a moment, I have the oddest impulse to slip my fingers soothingly through his hair, to trace my thumb along that divot notched in his forehead and smooth it away. "I shouldn't have cornered you about story time this morning and tried to guilt you into it. I'm...sorry, too."

"It's all right." He clears his throat. "And for the record, the CCTV footage streams to the bookkeeping room. I had my eye on things; if it had gotten out of hand, I would have been there immediately."

I stare at him, confused, as if a veil's been lifted, revealing a person I barely recognize but who's also strangely familiar, like looking at a face and knowing I've seen it before, nagging at the back of my brain.

"So—" he clears his throat. "What was with the weird moment with Luke? When you told him he'd played well? And he said that's high praise, coming from you. Do you play hockey or something?"

"Oh..." My instinct is severely to guard this part of my life, but I suppose if Jonathan's capable of an apology, I can be capable of a smidge of trust. "My dad's Nicholas Sokolov. Needless to say, I know the game pretty well."

Jonathan throws me a shocked double take before refocusing on the road. "That's not funny."

"It's not a joke."

He blinks slowly, stunned. "Explain yourself."

"Well, he and my mom met and fell in love, then they made a baby Gabby—"

"Gabriella," he warns.

I snort a laugh. "All right, I'll be serious. My dad wants a quiet life. All three of us do. We keep a low profile so we don't have to deal with the crowds. And I go by my mom's family name, Di Natale. It makes things easier."

Jonathan shakes his head slowly. "Holy *shit*."

Honestly, he's taking it better than most people do. He didn't swerve the car. He doesn't look about to faint. And he hasn't asked me for an autograph.

"That's why he never visits work," I explain. "Well, that's not true, I've brought in my parents after closing to show off the place, but not when we're open, because people can be so intense and they swarm you and ask for autographs and they just—"

"Ruin it," Jonathan says quietly. "Your ability to have an ordinary life with him."

I peer up at him. "Yeah."

He nods. "I'm sure he's very protective of that. And you. I would be."

"He is," I whisper.

"Well..." Jonathan clears his throat, eyes fixed on the road. "Your secret's safe with me."

I fiddle with the M&Ms bag, unsettled by how relieved I am that he knows the truth, how sure I am that I can trust his word. "Thanks, Jonathan. I appreciate that."

Quiet stretches between us until it's taut and dense. It's almost unbearable.

Until Jonathan tells Siri to play "Holiday Radio" with a note of command in his voice that's downright pornographic.

Now *that's* unbearable.

I gape at him. He glances my way, then does a double take. "What?"

"I've never heard your voice sound like that."

He arches an eyebrow. "Like what?"

"*Very* stern and bossy." I crisscross my legs against the ache that's nearly painful now. "Like...bedroom bossy."

He gives me a disbelieving side-glance. "I told Siri to play a music station, Gabriella, not get on her knees."

I choke on a fresh mouthful of M&Ms.

Jonathan stares at the road, battling a smile and barely holding his ground. "You have a filthy mind."

"*Me?* You're the one who just said—"

"Hush, you," he says, throwing my words back at me. "And enjoy this assault on the ears that I'm putting up with for your sake."

I snort a laugh. But my laugh fades as the song fills the car, the words hot and thick with meaning:

*I'll wait up for you, dear. Santa baby, so hurry down the chimney tonight.*

Jonathan clears his throat and rolls his shoulders, like his clothes feel too tight. I squirm in my seat, then crack the window. My cheeks burn.

"Hot?" he asks.

God, am I ever.

"A bit," I tell him.

Brow knit, Jonathan turns the dial down on the heat, then cracks his window, too. This horny song helps nothing. We're both flushed, eyes pinned on the road. I can hear each deep breath he takes, feel every thundering beat of his heart.

Maybe that's how I sound, too.

Panicking, I set my hands on my lap and discreetly play the song's chord progression, like my thighs are piano keys. It's a soothing movement that always calms me.

And while I settle myself, I walk through, step-by-step, what's happened since I got in this car. I am increasingly turned on and disoriented. The world feels like that Shel Silverstein poem, "Backward Bill"—upside down and unrecognizable.

Jonathan voluntarily drove me home. He bought mint chocolate M&Ms for me because he's sorry for how he acted this morning. He's playing holiday music for my enjoyment, even though he hates it. Either he has another personality he's been hiding for twelve months, or he's up to something.

I turn in my seat, facing him again. "Why are you being nice to me?"

His gaze remains fastened on the road, which is covered in snow. After a long, tense pause, he says, "I'm going to answer your question with a question."

"I don't like that."

"Too bad," he says, before a deep inhale. Then he exhales, thin and slow. "Why do *you* think I'm being nice to you?"

"Because you have a strategy. Some new angle for taking me down at work."

"And if I told you anything other than that, would you believe me?"

After a year of relentless mutual antagonism, the answer is out of my mouth before I consciously think it. "No, I wouldn't."

But for the first time since the day we met and chilly Jonathan Frost tipped my snow-globe world on its head, I wonder if maybe—just *maybe*—I'm wrong.

# CHAPTER 8

Over holiday music and my stealthy lap piano playing, Jonathan and I bicker the remainder of our way back to the city, disagreeing on which is the most direct route to my apartment that also avoids the worst traffic, right up until Jonathan smoothly parallel parks in front of my building. Because that's how life rolls for Jonathan Frost, even though I can count on my hand in the two years I've lived here how many times I've gotten a spot within even a block of my apartment.

I glare at him. "Seriously? Right in front of my place?"

He gives me a self-satisfied arch of one eyebrow, a wry almost-grin. "I have the world's best luck with parking."

"Of course you do," I mutter darkly.

Wrenching the car into park, Jonathan turns off the ignition, then stares at me, his throat working in a rough swallow. "I read that romance novel I bought at Bailey's."

I peer up at him, surprised, and...intrigued. "Oh?"

He nods. "It was good. It's not Austen, but—"

"Stop it." I playfully punch his rock-hard thigh, feeling a weird sense of déjà vu. "Stop baiting me!"

His mouth tips, so close to a smile, before it dissolves, leaving only silence and a thick, heavy charge in the air. Jonathan's jaw works. His eyes search mine. "They're very different," he says. "The love interests."

I nod. "Opposites, basically."

"But..." His gaze slips down to my mouth. "That ends up really working for them. It's the heartbeat of their connection, being drawn to each other's differences, stretching themselves to narrow that distance between each other without losing themselves. They...grow. Together. And more deeply into their true selves."

My heart's pounding, slamming against my ribs. Goddamn him for saying it so perfectly.

"Forced proximity also helps," I say, quieter, almost a whisper. "Being stuck in a carriage for days in a row, an inn with only one room and—"

"Only one bed," he says, his throat working with a fresh swallow. "I read about that. That's a popular trope. I can see why."

"Of course you read up on romance tropes."

"I read up on the whole damn genre." His fingers drum on the steering wheel. "I don't do things half-assed, Gabriella."

"No..." I search his face. "No, you don't."

Jonathan's hand flexes around the steering wheel. His jaw ticks. And then, suddenly, he throws open his door.

I blink, snapped out of a daze. Then I realize what he's about to do. Dammit. He's going to open *my* door next and be chivalrous again. I can't handle that, considering one hand clasp got me so worked up, I've been squirming in my seat the whole ride home.

I scramble for the handle, desperate to beat him to it, but he's already there, opening my door, then once again offering me his hand. I glance down at the mound of snow at my feet that I need to hurdle. Begrudgingly I take his hand and try to ignore the electric heat that jolts through me, radiating from where our hands are clasped to the tips of my toes.

Hopping over the snowbank, I land in the powdery softness with a thud, then peer up at the sky and Mother Nature's sugar dust drifting down on us. I hold out my tongue and smile.

Snow brings out the child in me. The wonder. I will never not love it.

A thick, cold flake lands on my tongue. I hum in pleasure, then slowly open my eyes. Jonathan's staring at me intently.

"What is it?"

"Your capacity for joy," he says quietly. "It's...humbling."

A compliment from Jonathan Frost. And not just any compliment—one that makes the heart of me feel seen and glowing, like candlelight spilling from a window on a dark, cold night.

My vision blurs with the threat of tears. My throat is thick. "You don't think it's silly?"

He shakes his head. "No."

"Odd? Strange? Juvenile?" I whisper. Just a sampling of the things I've been called when my happiness spilled over around those who found it to be "too much."

Taking a slow step closer, boots crunching in the snow, he holds my eyes. "No, Gabriella. I don't think it's silly or odd or strange or juvenile to hold on with both hands to the best parts of who we are when we're young and not let life take that from you. I think it's brave and badass and infuriatingly impossible not to admire you for it."

His knuckles brush my cheek, and my eyes begin to drift shut. It feels so overwhelmingly right, when all I can think is this is so absolutely wrong.

This makes no sense. Jonathan Frost isn't affectionate or tender. He doesn't read the shit out of a romance novel that I love or look at me with need burning in his eyes. He doesn't hold my hand or keep me warm or stare at me like everything he wants in the world is right in front of him.

And yet here he is—large rough hands gently cupping my face, close and calm and intent, his eyes on my mouth. *I need to kiss you,* his gaze says. *So badly.*

I stare up at him as his thumbs circle the dimples of my cheeks, as heat pours off his body, so close to mine that our thighs brush, our chests meet as we both draw in a deep breath. I feel this tug toward him in the pit of my belly, and dangerously higher up, where my heart thrashes against a tightening knot of something I'm too scared to even begin to analyze.

I have never understood something less—how much I want Jonathan, how deeply I ache for him. But maybe that's exactly why this needs to happen, to dispel the tension, to break the twisted bond of enmity that's braided us together the past twelve months. Maybe a kiss is all we need. And then I'll be free of this torture.

As I hold his gaze, he sees what I'm telling him: *I need it, too.*

My palms drift up his chest on a faint *swoosh* across the fabric. Jonathan peers down at me, dark lashes lowered over wintergreen eyes, that mouth that's so often tight and stern now lush and parted.

"I shouldn't do this," he says roughly, so quietly, I almost don't hear him. "Not yet."

I don't understand what he's saying, but I'm beyond sense, beyond thought. All I want is to be released from the torment that is wanting him, that's sunk its teeth into me, and make it let go. I'm going to kiss it right out of my system. It has to work.

Jonathan bends closer despite his words, as I press up on my toes, and finally our mouths brush, gently, then deep. I breathe him in, and it's pure exhilaration, like a gulp of bracing air while rushing down a snowy mountain. He tastes like rich chocolate and cool water and—Sweet Jesus—his tongue flicks mine and my knees give out. I throw my arms around his neck, thread my fingers through the thick, silky strands of his hair as his arms wrap around me until we're crushed together, chest to chest, hearts pounding.

Tipping his head, Jonathan deepens our kiss until it's hot and slick, a desperate dance that beats to the rhythm of *yes* and *more* and *don't stop*. His fingers sink into my coat, and he drags our hips together. I gasp, feeling him thick and halfway hard already, snug against where I'm aching and wet beneath my clothes. Our breathing's harsh and ragged, between each feverish, devouring slide and stroke of lips and tongue. I press myself against him. Our bodies rock together.

Jonathan's hands tighten around my waist and slide up my back, tangling in my hair as he kisses me so deeply, it's like our mouths are making love. I'm frenzied, wild, sucking his tongue, and he groans, rough and low in his throat, like there's no sweeter agony than this. A helpless moan leaves me, too. I sound devastated. Because I am.

Why is this the best kiss of my life? Why did it have to be him?

"It's too good," I whisper through the knot in my throat, the ache in my heart, even as I kiss him again and again. "It wasn't supposed to be this good."

"It wasn't, huh?" he says softly against my lips. "Of course you're roasting me. Even while we kiss."

*Kiss.* The word echoes in the snowy silence as reality hits me like a frigid slap of winter wind. I wrench myself away, shaky fingers brushing my lips. Oh my God. I kissed Jonathan Frost. More than once. In fact, many times. Passionately.

Jonathan looks at me like a haze has cleared for him, too. Like he's just processed what he's done, and can't believe he did it. Before either of us can speak—though what the hell could we even say?—I stagger backward, hurrying up the steps to my building's entrance. But for some inexplicable reason, as I reach the top, I turn back and face him.

Jonathan stares up at me, still breathing roughly.

I'm still breathing like that too, like there's not enough air, like the only air I want is each jagged breath stolen between kisses that unravel and tangle us together.

What an absolute disaster.

Frantic, I rush inside, then sprint upstairs to our second-floor apartment. Shutting the door, I slump against it and sink to the floor.

"What the fuck?" I whisper into the silence.

From where I sit, I can see straight down the hall to my bedroom and my desk, the laptop perched on its surface. I think of Mr. Reddit, and my stomach sinks. He's the one who I've been waiting for, the one I was supposed to kiss someday as snow fell from the sky.

No, we're not together, but we both more or less admitted we hoped for it, once we met and got to know each other in person. How did I lose sight of that? How did I let Jonathan's sultry wintry scent and his romance-novel spiel and his cozy car and his cache of mint chocolate M&Ms sway me so easily?

Sickening fear washes over me. What if I've waded into dangerously familiar territory with Jonathan?

I've been seduced for ulterior motives before, and while Trey was as different personality-wise from Jonathan as day from night—all sunshine charm and flirtation, compared to my cold, surly coworker—their aims are much too similar, aren't they?

Trey's ultimate goal was for his family's business to own Bailey's Bookshop, and in an attempt to secure that, he took advantage of my trust, my romanticism, my belief in the best of people. Jonathan wants the bookshop for himself, too, and he's proven himself ambitiously strategic and calculating. I'm not sure how this seductive campaign, this nice-guy routine and kissing me breathless, plays into his scheme, but what reason do I have to believe it's anything other than just that —a scheme?

Whatever Jonathan's motive for exploiting this sexual attraction that I can't deny any more than I can deny the curls on my head or the color of my eyes, I have to stop this. Right now. Not one more moment mulling over the longing in his gaze, that sexy almost-smile as he walked out of the locker room and saw me there. No more thinking about my perfect peppermint hot cocoa or his mint chocolate candy stash, or his appreciation for romance or his heartfelt apology...

Or those kisses. God, those kisses.

Then again...maybe every sweet, sensual thing that man squeezed into one small hour is *exactly* what I should be thinking about. Maybe it's time to use Jonathan Frost's weapons against him.

Stumbling upright, I run to my room and wrench open my closet door to search for the dress to beat all dresses. I unearth it, then hang it on the closet door, inspecting it with a tilt of my head. Gingerbread takes one look at the dress, then lets out a long meow.

"Agreed, Ginge. It's pretty *va-va-voom* for work, but you know what they say: desperate times call for desperate measures."

If Jonathan Frost thinks he's going to Lothario me right out of a job, he's got another thing coming.

I pump myself up as I steam-press the wrinkles out of every crimson panel of my dress and pick out the perfect pair of superbly festive earrings. I remember the fire in Jonathan's eyes as he told me, *I'm not walking away without fighting for this, Gabriella.*

I loathe myself for falling prey to his nice-guy act in the car.

I loathe myself for kissing him as much as he kissed me, for letting him hold me to his body, fierce and hot and hard, when he's not supposed to be the one I want.

I loathe that as I watch snow falling outside my window, all I see is snowflakes crowning his dark hair, and when I lick my lips, all I taste is that first intoxicating brush of his mouth and mine.

Flopping onto the bed, red dress pressed and waiting like a suit of armor, poised for battle tomorrow, I wrap Gingerbread in my arms and bury my face in her velvet-soft fur. She meows, peering up at me inquisitively.

"What's my plan, you ask?" I kiss her perfect pink nose. "I'm going to work tomorrow, and I'm bringing Jonathan Frost to his *knees*."

I caved last night and listened to my romance audiobook because I was desperately under-slept and I needed to be rested for my plan of attack. Unfortunately that led to another erotic aristocrats-in-the-library dream that put its predecessor to shame.

I can*not* think about it.

Not without blushing head to toe and remembering every place Fantasy Jonathan's hands and mouth were last night.

Which is why, as I power down the sidewalk toward the bookshop, I'm doing everything I can to distract myself. Mentally checking off my to-do list for the rest of the week, I have holiday tunes blasting in my headphones, and I'm relying entirely on my vision to ensure I'm not taken out by a car like a spare bowling pin. This means my headphones block out not only traffic noise but also the sound of approaching footsteps, leaving me fully unprepared when a hand wraps around my elbow.

I let out an instinctive shriek and drop my peppermint hot cocoa to the pavement as self-defense kicks in. I'm about to grab their wrist and, like Mom taught me, tug forward, then twist, but they let go of my arm before I can.

Just as I'm spinning around to throw the heel of my hand into their nose, the familiar scent of overpowering cologne wafts through the air and jogs my memory. "Trey!"

Blond hair, short on the sides, longer on top. Wide sky-blue eyes. He looks like a Ken doll who's been surprised.

Panting, I rip off my headphones and face him. "What the hell, Trey? You scared me!"

He opens his mouth to answer me, but it's not his voice I hear. It's Jonathan's.

"Gabby!" Holy shit. It's his Siri-get-on-your-knees voice. Commanding and deep and thunderously loud.

I'm speechless as I glance past Trey's shoulder, watching Jonathan sprint closer and closer.

Trey seems to sense he has very little time. "Gabby, listen to me," he says. "Bailey's days are numbered. Come work with me. Bring that small-store charm to Potter's. Independent bookstores are dying, almost extinct. All that's left is to bring what you love about them to the chain store experience."

I recoil from that. "That's not what I want. I want to save Bailey's."

"You can't," he argues, stepping toward me. "Don't be naïve. Your idealism isn't going to save—"

Thankfully, Trey doesn't get to finish that dismissive thought. It's cut off abruptly as Jonathan restrains him in one smooth motion, pinning him against the nearby building.

He could have body checked and brutalized him, but Jonathan's controlled, leaving Trey undamaged, only stunned, his breath rasping faintly beneath Jonathan's forearm. "Are you hurt?" Jonathan asks me, scanning me for signs of harm.

"I'm okay. He caught me by surprise and startled me, but he didn't hurt me. You can let him go."

Immediately, Jonathan lowers his arm and comes my way, ignoring Trey, who makes a big show of coughing and rubbing his throat.

Besides the fire in his eyes, the tight set of his mouth, Jonathan looks completely calm. He's not even winded. "You're sure he didn't hurt you?"

"I'm sure," I whisper, something thrilling and terrifying happening inside my heart. My ribcage is a club when the ball drops at midnight—glittering, glowing, effervescent.

"I wasn't trying to scare you, Gabs," Trey says, breaking the moment.

*Gabs.* God, I hate that nickname. Peeling my gaze from Jonathan, I glance his way. "And yet you grabbed my arm from behind?"

"I called your name a dozen times," he says patronizingly, as if this is somehow an oversight on *my* part. "You didn't hear me."

"Of course I didn't hear you!" I point to my headphones. "And I still don't want to."

"Well, what else was I supposed to do?" Trey says, giving me those pathetic pleading blue eyes he tried when I broke up with him. "I've tried calling and texting you from a handful of numbers, none of which went through after my first message. I wrote you notes. I sent you a bouquet. I said I was sorry and I missed you. I heard *nothing.*"

"That's because I blocked every number you used and because when I said we were over, Trey, I meant it! I'm done. And now I'm going to work. For the last time, leave me alone."

"Gabs," he begs, stepping into my space, "hear me out—"

"No, Trey."

"Please." He steps closer, reaching for me. "Just—"

Jonathan's hand lands with a hard *slap* on Trey's chest, then pushes him back until Trey can't reach me. His voice is black ice—lethal but dark and deceptively smooth. "She said *no*."

Trey glares up at Jonathan, then shrugs out of his touch, stepping back as he brushes off his douchey puffer jacket where Jonathan's hand is still imprinted in the expensive down fill. Peering my way, he scoffs. "What, is he your boyfriend now or something? The bookshop *help*?" The condescension he crams into one little word is astounding.

"Jonathan and I are co-managers, Trey. And while our relationship is none of your business, I'll tell you this much—he's ten times the person you are. Now fuck off, and have yourself a miserable little Christmas."

Storming past my piece-of-garbage ex, I start down the sidewalk. Jonathan falls into step with me, twice glancing menacingly over his shoulder, most likely to scare the hell out of Trey so he doesn't follow me. We don't speak as we walk the block between Bailey's and where Trey stopped me. When we reach the shop, Jonathan unlocks the front door, then holds it open so I can enter first.

"Thank you," I tell him quietly.

Before he can respond, I power walk to the back room, yanking off my mittens, unwinding my scarf, blinking away threatening tears.

Fucking Trey. Telling me that I'm naïve and idealistic. That I can't save this place. I'll show him. I *have* to.

There's a soft knock against wood nearby, and I know why. After my scare, Jonathan's being considerate, not wanting to startle me. Gone is my chilly, surly nemesis, and in his place stands someone who I told Trey is ten times the person he is.

And I meant it.

Because I simply cannot believe that Jonathan Frost would come running my way and throw himself bodily between me and the threat of harm, then turn around and try to seduce, swindle, or sabotage me out of a career.

Which, I realize, after all these months of hating his guts, is a profound relief. Despising someone is exhausting, and believing the worst in them is a burden to the soul. I didn't realize how tired it made me, until now, like peeling off frigid soaked clothes after a long day in the snow, I feel a weight lift, the warmth of tentative hope wrapped around me.

I'm not exactly sure what I think of Jonathan. Not yet. I only know that what I've thought of him doesn't fit what I just experienced. I know he stuck up for me and protected me and you don't do that for someone whose life and job you want to ruin.

Beyond that, I don't know what to think.

What I *do* know is this turn of events unfortunately takes the wind out of my sails with the wardrobe choice today. Now this dress isn't vengefully sexy. It's just...sexy. And I'm pretty sure after kissing each other the way we did last night, looking sexy for Jonathan Frost is a not-so-good idea.

"Gabriella." Quiet and low, Jonathan's voice dances like a lover's fingertip straight down my spine.

"Yes," I manage.

"Are you all right?"

Standing with my back to him, I keep my coat on and stare at the wall.

Am I all right? No. I'm not. My shithole ex just scared the hell out of me and defended his invasive behavior. Jonathan came running to defend me. And now I'm standing in the tiny back room with nothing but a wool coat keeping Jonathan Frost from seeing me in The Very Sexy Red Dress. I'm standing here, my heart pounding, because my world's rearranging, because despite my deepest desire to keep Jonathan Frost in the tidy box of enmity wrapped in a bow of prideful dislike, he punched a hole in that box last night, then obliterated it entirely this morning.

Now I have...nothing. Not enmity, not arm's angry length, not even a wool coat or a red dress or skin and bones, guarding my heart from him.

And I have to face that. I have to face him.

So, sliding off my coat, turning toward Jonathan, I do.

# CHAPTER 9

"**G**abriella," Jonathan says again, gentler, patient, as I start to turn and face him. "I asked if you're..." His voice dies off. His gaze slides down my body like it's beyond helping, before he shuts his eyes and drops his head against the doorway with an audible *thunk*. "Jesus Christ."

"It's a little much for work," I admit, staring down at the flowy red fabric, biting my lip. "Okay it's a lotta much for work."

Jonathan's so quiet.

"You okay over there?" I ask.

"I asked you first," he says through a tight jaw.

His eyes are still shut, his dark hair windblown and messy, a flush high on his cheeks. He breathes deeply through his nose, and his jaw tics with each breath. My gaze travels the evergreen V-neck sweater hugging his strong arms and broad chest, draping just a little at his waist, leaving me to imagine the pleasure of my hands traveling that soft fabric and the hard, unyielding muscle beneath.

His hands are fists in the pockets of his buckskin brown

slacks, tailored perfectly to a gloriously hard ass and long muscular legs, the classic powerful build of a hockey player. His polished brown boots wink under the store's lights. He looks as good as he ever has, no—better. He looks fine as hell.

I stare down at my red wrap dress, a soft flowy bow at the waist, a deep *V* neckline with a snap that holds it together at the swell of my cleavage. The bell sleeves and fluttery hem, paired with chunky heel boots, turn my not-so-substantial cup size busty, accentuate my wide hips, and make my legs look a mile long.

We both brought our seductive wardrobe A-games, and for a moment I wonder if Jonathan suspected me of the very thing I suspected him of, too.

What a pair we make.

"I'll be okay," I finally answer him. Jonathan hasn't opened his eyes. "Fair's fair. I answered. Now you."

He shakes his head side to side. Slowly, I walk toward him, each *clack* of my boots on the warm wood floors an echoing heartbeat. And when I stop, placing us toe to toe, I realize we're standing beneath mistletoe.

Slowly, Jonathan opens his eyes. But he won't look down at me. He stares up at the mistletoe hung above us, golden ribbon tied around it.

And for a moment, I have the ridiculous thought that I would love nothing more than to kiss Jonathan Frost until the end of time.

But even with my newfound confidence that he's not playing dirty, not attempting to Casanova me right out of my dress and into unemployment, our rivalry still stands. Even if we aren't the vilest of enemies like I thought we were, our goals are still fundamentally opposed.

And then there's my greatest reason of all. My online friend, the guy who's wanted to meet me for months, who I've wanted to meet, too. The good, kind, nerdy Mr. Reddit.

I can't let myself forget that. I can't daydream about kissing Jonathan Frost at work or in my bed or outside on a snowy day. I can't lust after him. Not when I have less than two weeks to kick his ass and close out the year with record sales. Not when Mr. Reddit's almost within reach.

Finally, Jonathan lowers his eyes until they meet mine. I have never seen someone try so hard not to stare at my breasts. "Miss Di Natale."

"Yes, Mr. Frost."

He glances back up at the ceiling. "You keep spare clothes here, don't you?"

"Yes. Why?"

"I need to know what it will take for you to change out of that dress, and into those clothes."

I snort a laugh. "But I'm comfy. I don't want to change."

He sighs like he knew I was going to say that.

"Unless..." I pop a hip and tap my chin, feigning thought.

He lowers his gaze until it settles on my mouth. "Unless what?"

"Unless...you forfeit a day of sales to me."

His eyes snap up and meet mine, fire flashing in them. "Back to that damn bargain of yours, are we?"

I shrug, hoping I look more nonchalant than I feel. My heart's pounding. "It's your bargain, too," I say coolly. "You agreed to it."

He laughs emptily, shaking his head. The arrogant condescension of his response trips a wire in me.

"I'm not sure what's so amusing about our bargain and what's at stake, Mr. Frost. Is the situation somehow beneath you? Am I being ridiculous, holding us to it? Maybe I'm supposed to set aside our understanding since we got a little carried away last night and because you stuck up for me this morning while I dealt with my creep of an ex—the same guy who, I'll let you in on a little secret, was the last person I made the mistake of trusting to have the best intentions and nearly sabotaged my career."

Jonathan levels me with the coldest look I've ever seen from those wintergreen eyes. "Perhaps, Gabriella, you might consider that not *everyone* is a morally bankrupt prick like Trey Fucking Potter. But of course, by all means, hold on to that bargain. Throw it in my face every moment we go anywhere beyond mere civility, and certainly don't let anything like the past twelve hours, let alone the past twelve months, get in its way."

He pushes off the wall and steps toward me, until our chests brush and we're face to face, sharing heated, livid glares. "God forbid you trust me," he says, "or think well of me or allow for the even slightest possibility that making you miserable and jobless isn't my life's calling. No matter what I do or say, Gabriella, you see only what you want: a villain."

"And why shouldn't I? Am I missing something? Did you or did you not come into this shop twelve months ago, level me with one cold, disdainful glance, and then proceed to systematically criticize everything I was doing wrong, scoffing at my—yes, I'll admit, somewhat chaotic—methods, and time and again poking a hole in my every creative idea for how to give this place a fighting chance because it wasn't a 'data-driven' approach? Did you or did you not agree to secure your place as sole manager here after the new year by outstripping me in sales?"

He leans in, voice low and dangerous. "Fine. I haven't been the warmest personality, and I might have come across as cold at first, but you have a very interesting recollection of the last twelve months, Gabriella. Because from where I'm standing, you spent the past year repeatedly perceiving practical changes in business operations as personal attacks, resenting me for doing the job I was hired to do, to make this shop more efficient and profitable, all the while—or so I thought, until quite recently—dating the fucking competition."

I open my mouth, but he presses on, his breathing harsh, his eyes burning. "As for your little 'bargain' over who ends up running this place, yes, I agreed. But you're forgetting a rather important detail, Miss Di Natale: this was *your* idea, *your* terms, *your* ultimatum. You never once considered a different outcome or solicited my opinion on the methods to achieve it. Because in your eyes, all we could ever be is spiteful, petty opposition." Leaning in until his breath is soft at the shell of my ear, his mouth so close, I could turn and our lips would brush, he whispers, "Who's the real villain here?"

Anger floods my body like lava, molten hot, burning through me. The audacity he has—

The jingle of the back door chime makes us wrench apart. Mrs. Bailey's humming to herself as she walks in, all smiles when she glances up. "Good morning!"

Both of us manage stilted *Good morning*s in response as she shuts the door behind her and shucks off buttery black leather gloves. Her smile falters as she peers between us. "Everything all right?"

Jonathan clears his throat and sets his hands in his pockets. "Just fine, Mrs. Bailey."

"Yep." I force a smile. "Just fine."

Peering up at the sprig of mistletoe hanging over us, she sighs. Then, without a word, she steps around us toward the bookkeeping room.

I'm still staring after Mrs. Bailey when Jonathan storms over to his coat hook, grabs his jacket and gloves, and is out the back door in a gust of arctic wind that follows in his wake.

While Mrs. Bailey deals with whatever bleak financial reality awaits her in the bookkeeping room and Jonathan remains strangely absent—not that I've kept an eye out for his return or anything—I stay busy.

My usual headphones on, I drown out the replay of Jonathan's embittered words, because if I think too long about them, I start to panic.

What if I was wrong about him? About us? About so much?

I push back against that growing fear and tune out the world with holiday music while I rearrange the window displays, redo the outdoor easel's chalk art, then send an email to our subscribers about the Big Sale Event on our last open day, December 23, featuring unprecedented discounts, the local bakery's best seasonal pastries, homemade holiday gift crafting, and live music.

When my stomach starts to spasm with hunger pains, I emerge from my deep focus long enough to wander into the break room and inhale a mint chocolate protein bar. I had all of two sips of my peppermint hot cocoa before Trey scared it right out of my hands, and I haven't had anything since.

Just as I'm finishing my last bite, Mrs. Bailey pops her head out of the back room and says, "Gabby, dear—my office, please?"

"Of course," I tell her, trying very hard not to catastrophize as I follow her into the bookkeeping room, where I'm met with the sight of a cluttered desk that makes Jonathan hive.

Gesturing to the chair across the table, she says, "Please have a seat."

I feel like I've been called to the principal's office. In which case, I want my partner in crime getting handed the same talking-to.

"Is Jonathan joining us?" I ask.

"I'm not sure Jonathan will be back. I called his cell phone and told him to take the day off if he needs it."

My stomach drops. "What?"

He'll lose a day of sales. And besides that, Jonathan's such a hard-ass, he only misses work if he's on-death's-doorstep sick. It's happened twice in twelve months, and he was gone a grand total of one day each time.

"I wouldn't worry," she says.

Except I am worrying. Because since he left this morning and despite my best efforts to distract myself, I've been replaying every word of Jonathan's tirade. The foundation I've stood on since the day he started here feels like it's crumbling.

What if I wasn't just wrong about my seduction suspicions? What if I've been wrong about Jonathan himself? What if the man I saw this morning, whose behavior upended my perception of him and our dynamic, isn't a stranger so much as someone I rarely saw?

But if that's the case, why hasn't he told me? I have never met a more direct person than Jonathan Frost. He pulls no punches, minces no words. He lobs brutal truths like darts, with no concern for how they stick when they sink into the bullseye of your hopes and dreams and the comforting familiarity of all you've ever known. Why wouldn't he set me straight sooner?

"Gabby." Mrs. Bailey removes her glasses and sets her elbows on the desk. "May I ask you something?"

"Yes, Mrs. Bailey."

"What makes you still see Jonathan as your enemy? I understand why you did, at first. He encroached on your routine, on our old way of doing things; he's proficient in the areas you aren't, just as you are strong in many areas he isn't, I'd like to add. But I'd hoped..." She sighs, tipping her head. "I'd hoped by now you two would be past quarreling. Especially with what we're facing now, I'd hoped you'd find a way to set aside differences and see...all the good that could be possible between you."

I blink back tears, the full weight of this bearing down on me as Jonathan's voice echoes in my thoughts.

*You never once considered a different outcome or solicited my opinion on the methods to achieve it. Because in your eyes, all we could ever be is spiteful, petty opposition.*

"It's so hard," I whisper, "when you've been taken advantage of in the past, when the most vulnerable part of yourself is exploited so deeply. It's difficult to trust, to open yourself up once more and give people the benefit of the doubt. It's terrifying to risk getting that wrong all over again."

Mrs. Bailey's eyes crinkle with concern.

I dab looming tears from my eyes and try to smile reassuringly. "I'm sorry. I'm fine, really. I shouldn't be saying this to you—"

"Gabby, dear, of course you should. I asked. I want to know." Mrs. Bailey's soft, weathered hand lands warm on top of mine. She squeezes gently. "What you said, about having your trust broken, being manipulated, this is about the Potter boy?"

The memory of this morning makes me shiver. Trey's unwelcome touch, Jonathan running toward me like nothing in the world was going to stop him.

And then those words. *Did he hurt you?*

Nodding, I wipe away tears. Mrs. Bailey knows what happened with Trey months ago, because I told her. She knows I had no idea who he really was, that as soon as I realized his true intentions, we were through. It was awkward and not my favorite conversation, telling her, but Mrs. Bailey was sympathetic and reassured me that she believed me. I still felt like shit about it for months. "That really messed me up," I whisper.

She nods. "It's understandable to be wary after something like that. And let's be clear, while Jonathan isn't nearly as...*sinister* as you perceive him, he's no saint, either. He and I have had a few conversations about his demeanor towards you as well as our customers. He's exacting and proud and impatient, and he could certainly stand to smile more."

"Try *ever*," I mutter.

Mrs. Bailey chuckles. "You're very different people. I knew it would be a rocky start, and it was. Throw in a few misunderstandings, some power struggles, slightly clashing managerial styles—"

"Slightly clashing?"

She smiles a little sadly. "I didn't count on how stubborn you two would be, how resistant to...giving each other a chance." For a quiet moment, Mrs. Bailey searches my eyes. Releasing my hand, she sits back. "What if you tried to be friends?"

"I'm sorry, *what?*"

"Often the best path forward is discovered one step at a time. It's a difficult journey from enmity to friendship, but not an impossible one."

*Friendship.* I taste the word on my tongue, trying it out. Friendship. Could I be...*friends* with Jonathan?

I allow myself to picture it, ending this long, bitter slog of the past twelve months on a dignified final bend in the road. Our heads held high, mutual respect and may-the-best-one-win, friendly well-wishes for the other as we part ways.

But then I think about how I feel when my hand touches his, when Jonathan's eyes lock with mine and there's heat on his cheeks and he's looking at me how he did after the business meeting, in the car, when we kissed, when we faced off this morning—intense, charged, fraught...

None of that is friendship to me. At least, not like any friendship I've ever known. But maybe that's all right. Maybe whatever friendship looks like for Jonathan and me, for this sliver of time before we part ways, doesn't have to look like any other friendship in my past.

Mrs. Bailey seems to read my mind, as if she knows a thing or two about what it's like to walk the line between longing and loathing and try to carve a safe path between the two, to find a smooth, mild middle way.

"It's worth a try, isn't it? In the spirit of the season?" she adds, a twinkle in her eye. "To have a little peace on earth here in Bailey's Bookshop?"

I envision proposing friendship to Jonathan, laying down my weapon first, extending my hand as I offer a truce. I remember how it felt, his hand clasping mine. My fingertips and palms turn hot, singed with memory.

Privately, I reflect that "peace," whether we turn out friend or foe, is the last thing I'll ever find with Jonathan Frost. But what I tell Mrs. Bailey is, "I'll try. I promise."

# CHAPTER 10

## PLAYLIST: "MAKE WAY FOR THE HOLIDAYS," LE BON

An hour later, Mrs. Bailey is gone and the store is forty-five minutes into being open. I've sold two romance novels, one cozy mystery, and—*gag*—three thrillers. The place is empty for the time being, and I'm on my way to make a cup of sugary, milky tea, when I notice the mistletoe fell from the archway leading from the register to the back room. Stretching on tiptoe, I tack it back up by its golden thread.

That's when the back door opens for Jonathan Frost and with him, a gust of winter wind. He shuts it quietly, then peers up beneath dark lashes, those striking wintergreen eyes locked on me. I lower to my heels as Jonathan walks down the hallway, a beverage cup decorated with snowflakes in each hand.

"I'm sorry," we say at the same time.

"Can we talk?" I ask.

Jonathan searches my eyes. "Yes."

I wrap my hand around the cup he's holding that smells like peppermint and bittersweet chocolate. Our fingers brush. "I think I could use some liquid courage first."

His mouth lifts at the corner, the shadow of a smile. "You're in luck then."

"Thank you." Glancing over my shoulder, I see the store is still empty. I peer back at Jonathan and tip my head toward the break room. "Is now okay? Do you mind?"

He shakes his head. "I don't mind."

I lead the way to the back room, hot cocoa in hand, and sit at the table, watching him set down his coffee, then peel off his gloves, finger by finger. He shrugs off his coat, and it slips past his shoulders, down his back, before he rakes a hand through his hair and tidies the windswept waves.

Sitting across from me, Jonathan takes his cup, which I didn't realize I'd wrapped my hand around. His thumb brushes my finger, a reassurance.

"Thanks again for this," I tell him.

"You're welcome, Gabriella."

I take a drink of my peppermint hot cocoa. Jonathan sips his coffee. We sit in silence, steam wafting from our drinks.

Until I find my courage and say, "I'm not excellent at reading people, and...recent events have led me to believe that for quite a while, maybe since you started here, I've been thoroughly misreading you. And because of that, I've maybe, potentially, been *slightly* more hostile than warranted." I clear my throat and extend my hand. "So, I want to apologize for that and propose friendship."

Jonathan's brow furrows as he glances at my hand.

Silence hangs, colder than the outside air that followed him in on his return. My hand starts to waver, as does my courage. But just when I start to retreat, he clasps it, his grip warm and strong. Relief rushes through me, glittering like sunlight on snow and tinsel on tree boughs.

Jonathan's thumb strokes the back of my hand as he says, "I appreciate that. And I'm sorry, too." His mouth tips at the corner. "I've also, maybe, potentially, been *slightly* more hostile than warranted."

"Friendship?" I ask. His thumb's driving me wild. I cross my legs under the table and focus on the matter at hand.

"Friendship," he says.

"Great." I wrench away my hand more abruptly than I meant to, but friends don't get horny from hand-holding, and I've got to get this under control. "Excellent. Friendship it is."

Tipping his head, Jonathan wraps his big hands around his coffee. I should get a sainthood for how I stop myself from staring at those long fingers and how they curl around the cup. "What you said, before I left—"

"That was harsh of me." My cheeks heat. "I got carried away."

"Gabriella," he says quietly, his foot nudging mine under the table. "Let me finish."

I nod and stare into my peppermint hot cocoa.

"What you said about how I behaved toward you when I started," he says. "You're right, and I'm sorry. I've never been good at softening blows, conveying hard truths in comforting words. I don't get emotional about these things, but you do. Deeply. And I didn't understand that or empathize." He stares down at his coffee and sighs heavily. "I regret that."

"Don't beat yourself up. We're very different people with very different visions for this place, Jonathan. I think, even on our best behavior, we were bound to clash."

He glances up, fastening his gaze on me. "What's your vision?"

I smile, because it's impossible not to when I talk about the bookshop. "I want it to keep its heart. I want it to be a community cornerstone that welcomes with open arms anyone who wants to come in. I want it to be personal, set apart from online and chain bookstores. I want to keep its soul." Searching his eyes, I ask him, "What about you?"

He seems to hesitate for a moment, searching for the right words, before he finally says, "I...want it to be an efficient, modernized business that's financially secure enough to survive, so that 'soul' you speak of has a home for as long as possible."

Hearing him say that, my heart does a double axel and sticks the landing, a joyful rush of relief.

"Cheers to that." I knock my cup gently with his.

After a moment of silence, Jonathan says, "Gear shift."

"Ready."

"What's with the red dress of torture, Gabriella?" He's doing that thing again where he's very diligently *not* staring at my breasts.

I laugh. "Oh, that. So, last night, after—you know—I convinced myself in a whirlwind paranoia that you were using your sexual wiles to seduce me out of the job."

His eyebrows shoot up. "What?"

"You had mistletoe motive, or so I thought—"

"What the hell is 'mistletoe motive'?"

"C'mon, Frost. Stay with me. Hanging mistletoe is a tryst trap, a sensual snare. Like your alleged motives. You tracking?"

He bites his lip and stares up at the ceiling. "Tracking."

"So, I figured you've got this seductive sabotage angle, driving me home last night, playing chivalrous with that sexy Darcy-offering-a-hand-up-to-his-carriage business—"

"Wait, *what?*"

"Making my legs all noodley, kissing me—"

"Hey, you kissed me, too," he points out. "We kissed each other."

"Fair. We kissed each other. That was a m-mistake—" I falter, because it's hard to call those incredible kisses mistakes, but they were.

Weren't they?

"The point is," I continue, "we kissed, yes, but everything leading up to it, that was all you. And I couldn't figure out why. So I assumed the worst. Until you proved me very wrong this morning. And now I realize that while we don't exactly gel in our personalities or managerial styles or bookstore visions, you haven't been out to make my life a living hell, and at certain angles I'm not too hard on the eyes, and so maybe you're a little hot for me, and sometimes a kiss is just a kiss."

He's silent, his eyes dark and intense. "I haven't wanted to make your life hell, Gabriella. And I'm not trying to seduce you out of a job." Jonathan stares down at the tabletop, tracing a whorl in the wood grain. "And you definitely aren't hard on the eyes, from any angle. But I'm not so sure about that last part."

"The kiss? Or, kisses, rather?"

He nods.

"I'm with you. I don't just kiss people to kiss them. I don't feel sexual desire for them out of the blue, either. Not until I feel emotionally connected. Which sort of stumped me at first, when I realized I was..." I clear my throat as a blush heats my cheeks. "Into you. I'm demisexual, and I've never wanted someone I didn't deeply like after growing close with them.

"But then I reasoned, while I haven't *liked* you very much for most of the time I've known you, Mr. Frost, I've forged a *bond* with you—our love for this place, our shared responsibilities, even the way I can predict what'll irritate you as much as what'll please your money-counting Scrooge heart. It's a deeply fraught bond, but a bond nonetheless. There's familiarity and ironically enough, a bizarre form of safety in our dynamic and its predictability. A sort of...intimacy. That makes you, unfortunately, fair game. But what about you?"

I swipe my finger through the whipped cream on top of my hot cocoa, slip it into my mouth, and suck it clean.

A low, painted sound leaves Jonathan, like he's quietly dying.

"What?" I ask.

He buries his face in his hands. "You have to stop doing that."

"I'm just enjoying my festive beverage, Mr. Frost. Come on, I want to hear your theory about the kisses."

A long, ragged exhale leaves him. "I've said about all I can manage right now."

"Why?"

Finally he lifts his head. With one soft swipe of his thumb across my lips, he sets my whole body on fire. "You have whipped cream—" He swallows roughly. "Right at the corner of your mouth. And I cannot focus on this conversation, especially one about sexual attraction, while you do."

A fresh blush sweeps up my throat and cheeks. A heavy silence hangs between us.

Slowly I dart out my tongue, wetting my lips until I taste another fleck of sweet, heavy whipped cream. "How about now? All better?"

"No," he says quietly, his eyes glued on my mouth. "Not at all."

My breath hitches in my throat. "Why not?"

Jonathan's gaze flicks up and meets mine. "Because I want to kiss you more than ever. And you want to kiss me, too. And, given present circumstances, that should not be happening. Not between...friends."

God, he's right. I shouldn't want to kiss him. Not when we've barely crossed from enmity to friendly territory, not when there's Mr. Reddit waiting for me at the end of this madness.

And yet here I am, staring at Jonathan and his mouth, remembering what it felt like to kiss him—the longing that flooded me with each stroke of his tongue, every deep, hot brush of his lips.

*Friendship,* the angel on my shoulder singsongs. *You've agreed to friendship!*

**Friends don't kiss like that,** the devil purrs on my other side, twirling her fiery pitchfork deviously between her hands. *Friends don't star in your steamy nighttime fantasies—*

Steeling my resolve, I lift my cup and offer a toast. "To friendship."

Slowly, Jonathan lifts his cup and clinks it with mine. "Friendship."

"To doing everything we can to save Bailey's. To selling as many books as possible, even if it's still in competition with each other. We can be professionally competitive but still friendly toward each other, right? We can agree not to fight anymore? Well, not fight *with each other*, but still fight for the store, because I am fighting for this. Bailey's is my world. I've never wanted to work anywhere else."

He's quiet for a moment. "I know that."

"Can't you go work somewhere else after the new year?" I plead, my elaborate toast abandoned. We set down our drinks. "You're so business savvy. Don't you want to crunch numbers in one of those skyscrapers downtown, make a lot of money, drive a brand-new SUV?"

He arches an eyebrow. "Wow, Gabriella. Could you make me sound any shallower?"

"I'm sorry." I hang my head. "You're not. I know you're not. I just feel like you could succeed anywhere. And I'm not like that."

Shifting so that one of his boots slides between mine, Jonathan knocks knees with me. "When you say, 'I'm not like that,' what does that mean?"

"It means..." I clamp my boots around his and nervously tap them. And then here they are, the words I've held back for so long: "It means I'm autistic. And finding work environments that suit my sensitivities, that play into my strengths, isn't as easy for me as it is for you neurotypicals. It means I'm not great with people, but with books, I'm better. Books help me make sense of others, and they help me make sense *to* others. They're my conduit, one of the best ways I can relate to people.

"There's never been a place where I've felt so sure that I'm doing exactly what I'm supposed to, that I'm right where I belong, as when I'm helping someone find the perfect book here at Bailey's, connecting with them over a character, introducing a child to the story that begins their love of reading, turning a world-weary cynic into a voracious romance reader."

Jonathan stares at me. Tentatively, his hand travels the table, and his fingers tangle with mine.

*Not a single word leaves his lips, but like our first kiss, his voice is in my head, so clear. I want to know. Tell me everything you want, or nothing, if that's what you want. I'm listening.*

"It means I don't have the most nuanced social awareness and I do best with very direct, honest communication," I tell him, a little quieter, suddenly aware of how much I'm confessing. "It means loud and sudden noises hurt not just my ears but my brain and startle me badly—that's why I wear my noise-cancelling headphones so much. It means I love to start my day with a hot cocoa and I often eat the same lunch, because routines are soothing and make order out of what feels like a very chaotic world.

"It means I have the same sweater dress in six colors, because finding clothes that are actually comfortable *and* work appropriate is harder than you'd think, and when I find a unicorn like that, I hoard it. It means music isn't just a pleasure for me, it's vital to my happiness. It means I'm trusting and literal and I've been underestimated and misunderstood more than my pride would like me to admit.

"And it also means that I'm a creative and a daydreamer, an artistically expressive person who pours herself into her passions and loves fiercely—the causes and people close to my heart—and does none of that by half-measures."

As I draw in a deep breath, finally unburdened, I hazard a glance up at Jonathan. His jaw is tight, his eyes on fire.

"I feel very vulnerable right now," I whisper. "Say something."

"I—" He swallows roughly. "I wish I'd known. And at the same time, I feel like I already know a lot of this, too." His fingers dance along mine. "I'm glad I know even more now."

I swallow nervously. "I realize that just because I've explained all this doesn't mean I'm suddenly necessarily easy to understand."

He tips his head, staring at me. "But I think I do understand you, Gabriella...at least, a little. I couldn't help but start figuring you out, spending so much time together."

"I don't feel like I've figured you out at all."

His mouth quirks. "I have an excellent poker face."

"It's rude." I start to pull my hand away, but he holds tight.

"It's a defense mechanism," he says. "I'm good at hiding the things you aren't. And maybe that sounds like an advantage, but because you've been yourself around me, in lots of ways, Gabriella, I've learned what you like and what you need. I've figured out that change stresses you and unknowns give you unbearable anxiety."

I stare at him. "You have?"

"That's why I didn't tell you about the business meeting a week in advance. I knew you'd worry. And I—" He cuts himself off with a sigh, rubbing his forehead. "I didn't want you to worry, so I figured I'd tell you the day before, but then the flowers came that day, and you dropped that bomb about

Trey, and it threw me off, and then the next morning, before the meeting—"

"I know." I squeeze his hand, still tangled with mine. "You planned to tell me that morning. But the Baileys got here early."

His gaze searches mine. "Do you...believe me now?"

I smile. "I do."

Relief washes over his expression. "Good."

Our gazes hold. It's so intense. So...oddly intimate. It's overwhelming. So I look away, staring down at his hand wrapped around mine, our fingertips brushing.

"Gabriella," Jonathan says.

I keep my eyes down, heart pounding. "Yes, Jonathan."

His thumb strokes the back of my hand. "Thank you for trusting me."

"Thank you for being safe to trust."

Jonathan slips our hands apart, then clasps his coffee again, spinning it in a slow, steady clockwise turn. "I suppose in the spirit of friendship, I could reciprocate and be...vulnerable, too."

"Don't sound too excited."

He gives me a baleful look. "I'm trying here, Gabriella."

"Sorry." I nudge his foot under the table. "I appreciate that."

He stares into his coffee. "I have type 1 diabetes. It's well-managed. But it still impacts me. It's impacted us. Sometimes, when I've been grumpy, when I've abruptly ended conversations and stalked off, it's been because I didn't feel well, or my alerts were warning me I was too high or low. Because I needed to check my blood sugar or have a quick snack or catch my breath and wait for the insulin adjustment to kick in."

So many moments that confused me over the past year

start to fall into place. "Story time with Eli. Was your blood sugar low?"

He nods.

"And in the car, when you ate your candy, it was low then, too?"

He nods again.

"Your phone, you track it somehow."

"That's right. I have an app that's connected to my CGM—my continuous glucose monitor—but I check my blood sugar with finger pricks using a glucometer, too. My CGM isn't foolproof and I don't like relying only on that. So last night for instance, I checked with the glucometer right before I left the locker room after my game, and I was a little low. When I knew I was driving you, I wanted to be sure I was up enough and safe behind the wheel, so I checked again in the car using the app and my CGM, and I was still lower than I wanted. Thus, the peanut butter cups."

He's still staring into his coffee like he's not quite ready to face me after that. I wonder if, like me and my reluctance to open up before today, he's been scared to be seen differently. I want him to know he's safe with me, that knowing this about him feels like I've been given a key to a room of his heart that very few are allowed in, and that's a gift I'll protect fiercely.

Knocking his boot gently under the table, I finally earn his eyes and give him the words of affirmation that he gave me. "Thank you for trusting me."

His eyes search mine, and he nudges my foot back. "Thank you for being safe to trust."

"You can tell me from now on, okay? When you don't feel well or when you need a break. Just like I'll try to be real with you, especially when I'm struggling." I pause for a moment, to try to find the words, because this matters and I want to say it right. "I know I don't *get* it, in the sense that I don't have diabetes, too, but...maybe I understand it a little, living with something persistent and beyond your control. You can't take it off or walk away from it or lay it down for a while. And even when you've become accustomed to its reality, when it's not really bad or good, it just...*is*, sometimes it's hard when you're with others. When you feel that sense of difference and distance from them as you deal with the part of yourself that they don't understand, that you have to think about in social situations and in your daily life in ways they don't."

Jonathan's quiet. But then his boots softly clamp around mine, our feet tangled under the table. "Thank you, Gabriella. That—" He clears his throat, and when he speaks again, his voice sounds different. Quieter, tight, like he's barely holding something in. "That means a lot to me."

Our eyes meet. We lean close. A little closer. Warning bells ring in my head. His thigh is right *there*, between mine. I'm staring at his mouth, remembering our every perfect kiss.

And thank God, right when I'm about to grab my *friend* by the gorgeous evergreen sweater and kiss him into the new year, the bell chimes over the door, heralding a customer.

# CHAPTER 11

## PLAYLIST: "THE HOLIDAYS WITH YOU,"
## SARA WATKINS

When the big Sale Event—also our final day open—arrives, Jonathan and I have successfully spent the past eleven days behaving ourselves. No petty squabbles. No arguing about whose turn it is to make the coffee and who made it too strong. No juvenile shelf-switching or feature-table rearranging to privilege our preferred genres.

No frantic, breathless kisses.

It's been devastatingly boring.

Except for the part where, as of yesterday's total that Jonathan ran—with my supervision, of course, to make sure there was no funny business when he crunched the numbers—our December sales totaled twenty-five percent greater than last year's and I am unequivocally in the lead.

I'm not exactly surprised, because while Jonathan's still hustled with customers to make decent sales, he's also spent a good bit of time frowning at his computer, shooing me away when I got too close. Every moment he was tap-tapping away on his laptop, I was out on the floor, logging more sales than him. A strategy that's had me a bit stumped. What's he been doing with that computer? I can't begin to imagine, unless he's started applying to those skyscraper downtown finance jobs, after all.

This should make me ecstatic. I should be running victory laps around Jonathan Frost to the *Chariots of Fire* theme. And yet, as I stare out at my bookstore kingdom, I feel no glory in my triumph. Instead, I feel very close to crying.

Which is absurd. This is what I've wanted—the bookshop safe, for now at least, my place in it secure. I've made peace with Jonathan, and we'll part on good terms. In just a few days I'll meet Mr. Reddit and hopefully feel every wonderful thing for him in person that I felt online.

So why am I on the verge of tears? What is *wrong* with me?

As I dab my eyes with the back of my hand, Jonathan joins me, hands on hips, surveying the store, which, I can admit, sort of looks like Santa's workshop and the Abominable Snowman had a baby and it just threw up all over the place.

Garland, tinsel, fake snow, sparkling homemade papier mâché and clay stars and snowflakes, kinaras, and dreidels, seven star piñatas, menorahs, and solstice symbols, as well as shiny silver and gold curled ribbons dangle from the ceiling and, let's be honest, all possible surfaces on which something can hang.

The air smells like powdered sugar and dark chocolate, citrus and fresh cut pine. Twinkly lights glitter across the tops of bookshelves, and iridescent metallic figurines decorate shelves and tables—reindeer, tiny gift boxes, and pine cones. The train set whistles softly on its tiny tracks, spinning around the base of the store's Christmas tree decorated in white lights and jewel-tone ribbon, garland and ornaments, nestled near the fireplace.

Colorful stacks of books brighten every table the store

owns, placing them front and center, within reach, garnished with clever little labels that list genre, tropes, themes, setting, and "If you like *Such and Such Title*, you'll love this." Beside the window display on one side is a massive table of pastries, which is next to another table of crafting supplies—cotton balls, paper plates, and glue to make snow people and winter animals like foxes, rabbits, and polar bears; gingerbread house materials; glitter and coffee filters to make snowflakes, finger paint and construction paper and colorful pipe cleaners to make any kind of festive craft a child could want, and pre-cut wood bookmarks for folks to decorate to their heart's content.

Sighing, Jonathan rubs his temple. "This is hell."

"It's not *that* bad," I tell him. At least, it won't be until we have to do clean-up after closing tonight.

"It is. And it will be even worse when your damned live carolers come."

Happiness swallows up my melancholy. It feels good to slip back into our old bickering routine. "It's a *jazz trio*."

There it is, that familiar disapproving arch of his eyebrow. "Who'll be singing Christmas carols."

"And lots of other wintertime tunes." I poke him in the ribs. "Don't be such a grinch. It's just a little festive fun."

"Festive fun?" He spins and stares me down, sending me stumbling back. But before my body hits the hard wood column behind me, Jonathan's hand slips around my waist, stopping me, wrenching me against him. For just a moment, we stare at each other and everything else...melts away.

Very deliberately, Jonathan releases my waist. But he doesn't step back. And neither do I. "Glitter, Gabriella," he finally says. "Hot glue. Confetti. Gingerbread. Sugar cookies. Icing... None of that goes with books."

I smile brightly. "Indirectly they do. They draw

customers, ingratiate them to the store, and compel them to buy our books."

Grumbling to himself, Jonathan turns away and stomps toward the back room. "I'm drugging myself. I have a headache already."

"It's good for business!" I call after him.

"I know!" he calls back. "And I still reserve the right to despise it!"

Laughing, I turn back and examine the main floor, then make some last-minute adjustments. Another pack of baby wipes on the pastry table—hopefully people will take the hint and clean their hands before touching books. The craft table closer to the front, so window-shopping passersby can see the holiday gift-making fun in action, along with the musicians, who'll be stationed in front of the other window.

The jazz trio arrives right on time, settles in, and has just finished warming up with the Vince Guaraldi *Charlie Brown Christmas* theme when I turn the sign to say *Open*. Not a minute later, a kid with dark hair bursts into the store, a woman with the same dark hair just past her shoulders chasing after him. "Jack!"

He freezes, hand hovering over the pastry table, specifically a massive chocolate cookie loaded with candy cane pieces. "What?"

"Slow down." Clutching him to her front, she offers me a weary smile. There's something faintly familiar about them both—their bone structure, their dark wavy hair. I can't place why I might know them, though. "Sorry for the explosive entrance," the woman says. "I'm Liz. And this is Jack." She peers down at him and arches her eyebrow, and *that's* familiar, too. "Who has something to say."

Jack peers up at me, looking sheepish. "Sorry I tried to grab a cookie."

"That's all right," I tell him as I crouch so that we're eye level. He seems like he's in elementary school, but tall for his age. Smiling, I offer him my hand. He smiles back, then gives my hand a firm shake. "I'm Gabby."

"Jack," he says. "Nice to meet you."

"Likewise, Jack."

He tips his head. "You like the holidays, huh?"

I wiggle my jingle-bell earrings and adjust my reindeer-antler headband. Jack eyes up the reversible white sequin snowflakes on my red sweater dress. "What clued you in?"

He laughs. "You're funny."

"Aw, thanks." I tip my head toward the pastry table. "If Liz is all right with it, you're welcome to have that cookie you wanted."

He glances up at her and earns her smile. "Mommy? Can I have it?"

"Yes, you may."

With his mother's approval, I pass Jack a small recycled-paper plate that I hand-stamped with snowflakes. Jonathan definitely almost burst an organ not teasing me for working on them every spare minute I had when a customer wasn't around, and the weirdest part is I missed his heckling.

Using the tongs expertly, Jack slides the cookie onto his plate. "Mint chocolate's my favorite," I tell him.

He grins up at me, mouth already full of cookie. "Mine, too."

His eyes wander the store as he chews his bite, and then they widen as he spots a book in the children's section that I keep on lower shelves so kids can access them. Gasping, he drops the cookie plate on the pastry table and runs toward it.

"Jack, wait!" his mom calls. "Use a..." He's already tugged the book off the shelf and dropped to the floor, flipping through the pages. "Baby wipe," she says helplessly. "We'll buy that, I promise."

"I wasn't worried in the least. Would you like coffee?" I

ask her, pointing to the carafes I set up. "Or tea? We also have hot cocoa and spiced cider."

Before Liz can answer me, Jonathan's voice cuts in, chilly as a blizzard. "This isn't a library, kid. You browse it, you buy it."

I whip around, scowling at him from across the store. "Jonathan Frost! Don't be such a Scrooge."

He arches an eyebrow at Jack, who's glaring up at him and says, "Bah humbug."

Rage pulses through me. I storm toward Jonathan, prepared to give him a piece of my mind. But suddenly Jack's face breaks into a grin, and he leaps from the floor, launching himself at Jonathan.

"Uncle Jon!"

Jonathan sweeps him up and hikes him high in his arms. "Hey, bud."

"Throw me!" Jack says. "Come on, throw me!"

Rolling his eyes like I've seen him so many times, Jonathan sighs. "Ah, I don't know."

"Do it, do it, do it!" Jack yells.

Jonathan tips his head side to side, like he's deliberating. Then, catching Jack completely off guard, he tosses him high up into the air, making his nephew shriek with happiness.

I watch them with a growing sense of panic. I can't take this, watching Jonathan so confident and capable with his nephew, playfully tossing Jack higher and higher, before hugging him tight. My heart's melting like hot caramel, warming every corner of me.

After one last toss that earns his nephew's shrieking laughter, Jonathan sets Jack on the ground, not the slightest bit winded, a faint flush of pink on his cheeks the only clue he just threw a sixty-pound kid into the air a half dozen times. Our eyes meet.

"Liz, Jack," Jonathan says, eyes on me as he wraps an arm

around Jack's shoulders, "I'm assuming you've met Gabriella. Gabriella, this is my sister, Liz, and her son, my nephew, Jack. Who I did *not* know were coming."

He gives her some kind of censorious sibling glare, but Liz only grins at him, a look that's downright disarming. She has deep, long dimples in both her cheeks, and her dark blue eyes sparkle. It makes me wonder if Jonathan becomes even more stunning when he smiles, too.

"We've met," Liz says. "Gabby was very gracious about our less than smooth entrance."

Jack tells him, "She gave me a cookie and let me look at books. And she's really pretty, just like you said—"

Jonathan's hand claps over Jack's mouth, his cheeks turning an even deeper pink. "Ever heard of a secret, Jack?"

"I warned you." Liz steps in with a baby wipe and cleans her son's hands. "Don't tell him anything you don't want him to repeat."

"He asked," Jonathan mutters defensively, pointedly not meeting my eyes. "What was I going to do, lie?"

Jonathan's mentioned me to his family? He thinks...I'm pretty? I mean, we've kissed each other, so I suppose I knew he found me attractive, but there's something different about hearing it, about seeing the way he looks at me now, serious and a little shy.

He glances away.

"We're going to look for a few more books, with *clean* hands," Liz says, taking Jack back to the children's section and leaving the two of us alone. The jazz trio's rendition of "The Christmas Song" plays softly in the background as Jonathan and I stare at each other.

"He's really sweet," I say quietly.

Jonathan throws his nephew a glance and buries his hands in his pockets. "He's a chaos demon."

It's so his humor, so obviously a deflection. I wonder how

often dry wit has covered what Jonathan really feels. "You love him. He's got you wrapped around his finger."

He glances back my way. "Unreasonably so."

"Lucky him," I whisper.

Jonathan's eyes hold mine. The jazz trio's music fades as the song ends, leaving a new, weighty silence between us.

But then the upbeat melody of "Ocho Kandelikas" colors the air, and the door opens to a rush of customers, the silence trampled by their arrival.

I'm tying a sparkling silver bow around a recycled paper bag stamped with Bailey's Bookshop logo when I sense Jonathan behind me, big and warm, smelling like woodsmoke and Christmas trees.

My customer senses him, too, and looks a little intimidated.

"Thank you for your business," I tell them brightly as I set the receipt inside the bag. "Don't forget to fill up on a complimentary hot beverage before you head outside, and have a happy holiday!"

I spin around and face the grinch behind me. He's scowling.

"Turn that frown upside down, Jack Frost."

His scowl deepens. "Have you stopped since the place opened?"

I scrunch my nose, thinking. "Maybe?"

"Eat." He sets a chocolate cookie with candy cane chunks on the counter, takes my elbow, and plops me on a stool. "And drink that." He points to a big cup of ice water.

"Wow." I'm already chewing the cookie. It tastes like heaven. "This is incredible."

He pastes on a polite almost-smile for the next customer

whose books he's started ringing up and says over his shoulder, "Cardboard would taste incredible after how long you've gone."

Warmth floods me. "Have you been keeping an eye on me?"

"Absolutely." He starts scanning the next stack of books. "You're not passing out and leaving me alone in this glitter-bomb hellscape."

I snort a laugh. "Ah, c'mon, Frost. It's not that bad."

He arches an eyebrow, slipping the customer's card into the chip reader and throwing me a stern glance. "Drink your water, Gabriella."

"So bossy," I mutter into the cup before draining it in one long gulp.

I get a grunt in response.

"There you are!" Eli's voice comes from right behind me. I spin around and see him, shoulder to shoulder with Luke and June.

"Look at you two," Luke says, sighing happily as he admires Jonathan and me. "The portrait of professional bliss."

Jonathan gives his friend a death glare while Eli and I hug hello. Before I can unpack exactly what's happening, June throws her arms around me next. "The place looks great," she says.

"Thanks," I whisper, hugging her back. "Um. So." I clear my throat as we pull away and throw a thumb over my shoulder. "Don't dismember him, but this is Jonathan Frost. Jonathan, this is my dear friend, June Li."

June peers up at him, and it's quite a journey, seeing as June is 5'2" on a good day and Jonathan's well over a foot taller than her. She gives him a pursed lip, blank look. "Hm," she says.

"We have a truce," I tell her out of the side of my mouth. "Remember?"

Eli sighs. "June. Be nice. It's the holidays."

"Bah humbug," she mutters.

Jonathan arches his eyebrow. "That's my line."

June's mouth twitches. She's fighting a smile. "So long as you're treating her like a queen now," she mutters, sticking out her hand.

Jonathan takes it and gives her a firm shake. "Doing my best."

"He's been a gem," I tell her. "He brought me cookies and hydration."

June nods. "I approve. She neglects herself."

"See?" Jonathan says to me, sounding annoyingly vindicated.

"Hey." I glance between them. "I get distracted sometimes. I don't *neglect* myself."

"What do you call not eating for six hours straight, Gabriella?" Jonathan folds his arms across his chest. "Hm?"

"Trust me," Eli says. "We know all about it."

"Okay." I hop off the stool and shove the last of the cookie in my mouth. "Enough of Gang Up on Gabby Hour. I'm taking June for a tour of the place."

Eli pouts. "What about me?"

I shoulder him playfully. "You saw it already for story time. Go browse with your honey. Oh, and Frost."

Jonathan's watching me intently. "Di Natale."

"Don't even try to steal my sales. Ring 'em up, fair and square, promise?"

His mouth lifts in the faintest whisper of a smile. "Scout's honor, Gabriella."

"Good." Dragging June with me down the hallway, I yank her outside to the back alley and slam the door behind us.

June frowns. "I thought I was getting a tour."

"I'm freaking out."

Her eyes widen. "Okay," she says slowly. "About what?"

"About Jonathan. And Mr. Reddit. It's like—my brain is this giant knot of tangled up Christmas lights, and I can't tell what's lighting up for who, and I feel guilty because it's like I'm betraying Mr. Reddit, and I feel scared about Jonathan because this is all so new, being friends with him, but somehow it doesn't feel new at all, and I'm weirdly happy around him and—"

"Woah." June sets her hands on my shoulders and squeezes. "Deep breath, Gabby."

I suck in a breath.

"And out," she says calmly.

I exhale.

"Good. Now." She yanks open the door and drags me back inside. "It's cold as Satan's balls out there. Let's go find a closet to talk."

"But it's hot in hell."

"Not according to Dante," June mutters, guiding me ahead of her. "Find a closet, would ya? In Dante's *Inferno*, Satan's frozen up to his waist, his wings beating furiously, but ironically that just keeps the lake frozen. The innermost circle of hell is self-sabotage...and balls that are blocks of ice."

"Wow. I forgot about that." I open the closet door where we keep janitorial supplies and lunge over a box of industrial-strength cleaner. June follows behind and shuts the door.

"Speaking of self-sabotage," she says, rounding on me. "Sit."

I sit. "I'm surrounded by bossy pants."

"Someone's got to balance out Eli," she says, nudging items off a box of toilet paper until it's clear for her to sit on. "He's too nurturing. Listen." June leans in, elbows on her knees. "You need to cut yourself a break. You're busting your ass at work, trying to save this place. It's your last day before holiday break, you're crushing it, and you're spending the day beating yourself up about a guy you've never met in real life and a guy you've hated for nearly a year and just started to be civil with. You owe them nothing, Gabby.

"If this Mr. Frost, who actually keeps an eye out for you and makes you happy, ends up being your person, then that was how it was meant to be, and Mr. Reddit was someone who was right for you at one time and not the other, and that's okay. If, once you meet Mr. Reddit in person, you realize that while you have an intense bond with your coworker after close quarters the past twelve months, the bond you and Mr. Reddit built over nightly chats has forged something much deeper, then that will be what you were meant to figure out and *that's* okay. Or they might both turn out to be assholes I have to beat up, and I will, and that will be okay, too."

"June. No assault."

"Fine," she grumbles, "but only because it's the holidays." Her eyes search mine. "My point is, you're too damn hard on yourself."

"But this doesn't make sense!" I moan, scrubbing my face. "It's confusing, and I'm emotional and—"

"Hey." June wraps her arms around me as the first tears spill down my cheeks. "Let's just take this one hour at a time, okay? You're doing great."

I pull away and wipe my eyes. "You think?"

"I know. You should be really proud of what you did out there. It's gorgeous. It's busy. You've poured your heart into this place, Gabby, and it shows. So let's celebrate that. Today, focus on your incredible professional achievement here. Three days from now, we'll deal with Mr. Reddit. After that, we deal with tall, dark, and surly out there. Now—" Standing, she straightens the black beanie she's wearing that nearly blends in with her sable locks. "Time for you to give me an actual tour."

June and I slip out of the closet, into the bookstore, and

my heart does a twirl of joy. After hours of being immersed in the busyness, I see it with fresh eyes—twinkly lights and jewel-tone ornaments, sparkling decorations and polished wood and row after row of rainbow spines. Customers sipping from steaming cups, kids and adults alike making crafts, the jazz trio with a small cluster of patrons dancing by the door. It's everything I hoped it could be.

Then I glance toward Eli and Luke who stand beside Jonathan at the register in conversation with the Baileys. This is beyond what I could have imagined, but it's so right—all of it, all of *us*, together.

Mrs. Bailey catches my eye and winks. I smile at her, before taking June for the grand tour.

Each step I take, I feel Jonathan's eyes on me. As I greet new customers, answer others' questions. As I break away from June long enough to stretch on tiptoe and reach my favorite holiday romance because it's just what this one customer needs. By the time we make our way back toward the register, when June's finally seen it all, my heart is flying, curving the bend of what I don't know, before it leaps into the air and spins and spins—

I glance up, knowing I'll meet his eyes, and I do, as my heart lands, safe and sure. This is what it is, to be caught in Jonathan's gaze, to be held, warm and steady: a gift.

One I'm terrified I won't get to keep.

# CHAPTER 12

## PLAYLIST: "HAVE YOURSELF A MERRY LITTLE CHRISTMAS," BIRDY

"**M**iss Di Natale." Jonathan shuts the back door behind him after his last trip to the dumpster, locking up for the night.

I drop into one of the wingbacks in front of the fireplace, groaning as I toe off my boots. "Mr. Frost."

Walking my way, Jonathan peels off the name tag that I stuck between his shoulder blades hours ago and holds it with thumbs and forefingers. "How long have I walked around with my front name tag saying, *Mr. Frost*, and my *back* name tag saying—" He pauses for dramatic effect. "*Actually, it's Mr. Grinch.*"

I bite my lip. "That would be...after you poached the couple from me when I was about to sell them the romance series box set—"

"I did not poach." He crumples the name tag, tosses it into a waste basket without even watching it land, as if he's so sure it will—which, annoyingly, it does—then drops with a groan onto the chair across from me. "I pivoted. You made your sale, then I made mine. They bought the romance box set—"

"And half of Stephen King's backlist."

Jonathan sighs as he stretches out his long legs and crosses them at the ankles. His head falls back against the chair, exposing the long line of his throat, the prominent jut of his Adam's apple. He looks gorgeous. And like he worked his ass off to make my big Saturday sale idea a reality.

It makes me feel a smidge guilty for my juvenile move.

"Sorry about the name tag prank."

His eyes stay shut. "It's fine. I slapped one on your back hours ago, too."

I gasp. "What?" Feeling for the name tag, I first try over my shoulder, then underneath. It's in the one spot I can't reach. "I can't get it."

His mouth twitches in another thwarted smile. He opens one eye and glances my way. "That's the idea, Di Natale."

"Get it off, you meanie." I cross the small space between our wingback chairs and turn so my prank name tag faces him.

It's quiet for so long, I glance over my shoulder. Jonathan's staring up at me, firelight bathing his face, turning his eyes dark.

Slowly, he straightens in the chair, uncrossing his legs, then bracketing me inside them. He sets his hands on my hips and coaxes me back. One hand stays on my waist, while the other slowly peels off the name tag. And then he sits back with it, crunching the name tag into a ball.

"Not fair!" I yell, tugging on his hand. Jonathan tugs back.

It sends me tumbling into his lap. Air rushes out of him. "Christ, woman," he groans. "You just pulverized my liver."

"Sorry," I mutter halfheartedly, freeing the balled-up name tag from his hand and carefully tugging it apart. The backing isn't very sticky anymore, after a long day on my fuzzy sweater dress, so after a few careful maneuvers, it's wrinkled but open, its words reading, *Off-Limits Under the Mistletoe.*

I give him a flat look. "Wow. Way to smash the patriarchy."

"I saw no less than five people hit on you today. I was just trying to convey that you're here to do your job and enjoy yourself, not fend off unwanted advances."

"Who was hitting on me? I didn't even notice."

He gives me a withering look. "Don't pretend you don't know, Gabriella."

"I'm serious! I can't tell when people are flirting with me."

He stares at me for a moment, his expression tense, before he clears his throat and says, "Well, trust me. They were."

"Hm." I stare at the name tag. "So he's sabotaging my sales, after all."

"You sold me under the table today, and you know it."

"Yeah, I did." Leaning in, I whisper, "So. Many. Children's. Books."

His gaze dips to my mouth. That's when I realize I'm in his lap still, our faces mere inches apart. I lean a little closer. Jonathan does, too. And it feels like a tear down the center of me, an awful, aching tug-of-war.

I'm meeting Mr. Reddit three days from now—Boxing Day, outside the Winter Wonderland display at the conservatory, 10:00 a.m. sharp—a plan I picked from among the ones he proposed in our Telegram chat, as promised. I've been counting down the days, both excited and nervous that we'll finally meet.

But it's harder now, to remind myself that I'm holding out for Mr. Reddit, the unlikely friend I found, who I've hoped might become more, when Jonathan Frost and I are seconds away from kissing each other.

*Stay strong, Gabriella!* the angel on my shoulder whispers.

Before the devil on my other side can chime in and tempt

me, I spring out of Jonathan's lap and fuss with the sequins of my snowflake dress. "Do you want a cup of tea?"

Jonathan sits upright, too, and clears his throat. There's a flush on his cheeks. "A cup of tea?"

"With a splash of whiskey. I think we earned it."

"Ah, so you too know that Mrs. Bailey keeps it in the cabinet for when she has to do month-end financials."

I laugh. "Before you came, that whiskey bottle made an appearance, often in our tea, at least once a week."

"Sure. Then let's have tea."

Jonathan goes to stand, presumably to contribute to tea-making, but I gently clutch his shoulders and push him back. "Sit. You did so much to make today happen."

"So did you," he says. "I can help."

"Don't argue with me for once, okay, Frost? You did a ton. Now let me make tea."

"I'll keep you company, at least," he says, gently clasping my elbows and guiding me back so he can stand.

After traipsing together into the back room, I prepare tea in the kitchenette while Jonathan digs around in his messenger bag, pulls out his glucometer, and does a finger prick as he sits at the breakroom table.

Seemingly satisfied with what his glucometer has to say, Jonathan packs up his kit and stashes it in his bag. He steps close behind me. "Sure I can't help?"

It's so unbearably pleasurable, his voice low and quiet, his big body right behind me, I nearly burn myself, pouring tea. I want to lean into him, let my head fall back against his shoulder and feel his arms wrap around me. "N-no. I've got it under control."

He seems to hesitate for a moment, like he's weighing... something. But whatever it is, it passes. Without another word, Jonathan strolls back toward the fireplace, then drops onto the wingback with a sigh.

"How ya feeling?" I ask, stealing a glance at him as I doctor our teas with whiskey.

He lounges in the wingback like a king on his throne, one long leg stretched out, an arm thrown behind his head. Firelight paints his face, the long line of his nose, the hollows of his cheeks. Our eyes meet, and he tips his head, examining me. "Fine, Gabriella."

I stare at the dark waves of his hair, his cool green eyes and long nose. Sharp cheekbones and lush mouth. And yet, for all his severe handsomeness, there's something softer about him as he looks at me, as I look at him.

Two cups of Darjeeling in hand, with a splash of milk and whiskey in each, I walk carefully back to the chairs and pass him his. "I put a sugar cube and a peanut butter blossom on the saucer. Not sure if you could use a little boost or not right now."

"Thank you." He takes the cup from me and forgoes the sugar cube but bites into the cookie.

Sitting across from him, I tuck my legs underneath me.

We drink our tea and crunch on our cookies in silence, staring into the fire. Until I glance his way and notice Jonathan's watching me. "What is it?"

He stares at me for a moment longer before he drains his tea, then sets it aside and says, "The numbers are in. Congratulations, Miss Di Natale. You won."

My stomach sinks. "I don't want to talk about that."

"Why not? You should be proud, Gabriella. You outsold me. Not that I ever doubted you would."

Tears blur my vision. It feels like an ice pick puncturing my chest.

I drain my tea, hoping it will thaw the chill spreading through my body, but I don't even feel the whiskey burn its way down as I blurt, "You're not quitting for sure, right?"

Jonathan examines me carefully, hands interlaced across his stomach. "Those were the terms of our agreement."

"What if I've changed my mind?" I whisper around tears thickening my throat. "What if I wanted you to stay?"

He's very still. Very quiet. Until he finally says, "You'd want that?"

I stare at him, tearing deeper inside myself. Should I want Jonathan around? When I'm drawn to him, when I miss our bickering, and I wish I could kiss him again, when I'm meeting Mr. Reddit, the friend I've hoped could become more?

Words catch in my throat. I don't know what to say. I don't know what I want. I feel like I'm falling apart.

"I—" The words catch in my throat, until they finally spill out. "I'm torn."

"About what?" Jonathan asks quietly.

I glance away, staring into the fire. "Because whatever's going on with us...it's messing with me. And there's someone I care about, but it's...complicated. Right now, we're just friends. That's all we've ever been."

"Friends," he repeats softly.

"I hoped maybe we'd become more, and I think he's hoped so, too, but now—" I blink away tears. "I don't know what I hope or think. We've never met in person before. We've only ever talked online. I mean it's been over a year, so I feel like I know at least parts of him very well, but that's not the same as knowing someone in real life, is it?"

He rubs his knuckles across his mouth. "How did you meet?"

"You're about the only person who I don't have to preface this with, 'don't laugh,' because you don't seem to possess that bodily impulse, but I met him on a nerdy bookish Reddit thread. He's...perfect," I tell him bleakly. "At least in our chat he is. And in that chat, I'm perfect, too. There's no real-life tension, barely any of my autistic traits foregrounded to trust him with and hope he's gentle toward. I've told myself it's this magical thing, how well we get along, but that's not reality, and I know I've been hiding behind a screen, hiding from being fully known and loved for all of who I am. Which is why I told myself I was going to be brave. And now I have plans to meet him in person."

"When?" Jonathan says, voice soft and dark as a midnight snowy walk.

"After we close for the holidays. Three days from now."

The hand in front of his mouth tightens to a fist. "Where are you meeting him?"

I give him a look. "Don't even think about playing security. I already had to talk down June, who's insisted on coming. We've agreed that she's allowed to observe from a discreet distance. She watches too much *Criminal Minds*—"

"Gabriella," he says, eyes pinning mine as he repeats himself. "Where are you meeting?"

"The Winter Wonderland display at the conservatory."

Jonathan's fisted hand drops to his lap, his gaze fastened on me. "Sounds like something you'd love."

"It is," I admit. He holds my eyes so intensely, I start to shift uneasily in my chair. "What about—" I fight the roar of jealousy clawing through me. "What about you? Is there someone?"

"A...friend," he finally says. "She's someone I met online, too, actually. A pen pal of sorts."

I smile. "Really? Have you met in person?"

"No." He glances away, staring into the fire. "Not yet."

Gently, I nudge his knee. "Why not? Mr. Frost, what do you have to hide about yourself behind the trusty protection of online chatrooms?"

He rolls his eyes. "Let's see. A less than warm and cheery

first impression. Black moods, especially around the holidays. Avoiding the 'I have diabetes' talk."

"Please. You have a grinch façade, but underneath is a heart of gold. And as for your less than cooperative pancreas, if she gives you hell—" I mime a one-two punch. "Lemme at her."

I don't even think he sees me. He's lost in thought, staring into the fire still. "What happens," he asks quietly, "when you meet and... What if he's not how you pictured him? What if he's the last person you expected?"

"I don't know. I just wish I'd met him months ago, and this wouldn't be an issue. I wish we didn't have this built-up idealization that we'll have to unlearn and work through."

"So you *wish* you knew the messy truths." His gaze snaps my way. "The hard-to-love parts of him."

"Don't you? Don't you feel that way about her?"

His eyes search mine. "Yes. So much."

"Then be brave," I tell him, closing the distance between us and squeezing his hand, torn as I struggle against the unreasonable possessiveness I feel for him. "Promise me you'll meet her, and when she meets you, she'll be lucky enough to see the real you, *all* of you, Jonathan Frost."

Staring at me, he's quiet for a long moment before he flips his hand and squeezes mine back. "You think she'll like that?"

"Jonathan. You're a grumpy curmudgeon, but you're also one of the best people I know. You've devoted yourself to this place. You'd do anything for the Baileys. You've been a good friend to me the past eleven days and an exceptional co-manager. You love your nephew so hard, seeing you two together made my ovaries do calisthenics—"

"Made them do *what*?"

"Shh, I'm being poetic. Let me pep-talk you. You're a rock star uncle *and* brother—you went and cleaned off your sister's car before they left because it had snowed, I saw you. You're smart and have the driest humor of anyone I've ever met, and if you're anything like in my sex dreams, you're an amazing lover—oh my GOD, I just said that."

I clap both hands over my mouth.

Jonathan's eyes widen. "What did you just say?

"Nothing." A blush heats my cheeks. A blush like I see heating his cheeks, too. "I should go."

Standing, I turn off the gas fireplace, escape to the back room, and start to bundle myself up for the walk home. I have to get out of here, before I say or do anything else to shatter this fragile, lovely thing we've built.

Friendship.

But then I feel him behind me, warm and close. So temptingly close. "Gabriella—"

"What I meant to say," I whisper, in the semi-darkness of the store, facing away from him. I scrunch my eyes shut and take a deep, steadying breath. "Was that if she's worthy of you, she's not going to *like* knowing all of you, Jonathan." I turn with his coat in my hand and set it gently in his arms. "She'll love it."

Jonathan slowly tugs on his jacket. I slip on mine. It's not until I've pulled on my mittens that I realize I forgot to button my coat.

"Dammit," I mutter.

Jonathan brushes my hands away as I start to remove my mittens and steps closer, deftly buttoning each one. He looks more serious than ever, eyes on his task, and I watch him with a knot in my throat. I breathe in his wintry woods scent and soak up the sight of him. "When will I see you?"

He fumbles with a button. "Soon. There's a lot to work out with the store."

"Okay," I whisper.

His mouth tips at the corner. "Gonna miss me, Di Natale?"

"Like I miss an abscessed tooth."

His mouth tips a little more. It's the closest to a smile yet. "Good."

And then we step out into the snowy world. Jonathan locks up, mouth pursed as he concentrates before he says, "I'll walk you home."

"Jonathan, you don't have to."

"It's late, and it's not safe for you to walk alone." He turns and then gently clasps my headphones from where they sit around my neck, nestling them on my ears. "We don't have to talk," his muffled voice says. "We can just..." He peers out at the snow, then tips his face up to the sky.

"Be," I finish for him.

He peers down at me, his eyes warm. "Yeah."

And we do just that, long, quiet strides along the snow-packed sidewalk. Elbows bumping, eyes dancing each other's way. I hum to myself, and Jonathan is silent, staring ahead, a soldier marching into battle. He looks so serious, and I wonder what's heavy on his mind. But I don't ask. Because I shouldn't want to know. I shouldn't want to drag him inside my apartment and warm him up and ask him to pour out his heart.

As we stop in front of my building, I turn and face Jonathan. "Thank you for your escort, good sir."

He gives me a stern look. "You have no business walking alone, especially with those headphones on, understand?"

I shrug. "It keeps life exciting."

"Exciting." He massages the bridge of his nose. "Christ, Gabriella."

Carefully, I step close and smile up at him, blinking away snow and the threat of tears. "Happy holidays, Jonathan."

To my absolute dizzying delight and bittersweet astonishment, Jonathan wraps me in his arms and sets his cheek on the crown of my head. A long slow exhale leaves him. "Merry Christmas, Gabriella."

We pull apart, setting necessary distance between us as I tell him, "Promise you'll meet your online friend, okay?"

He nods. "I promise. And you, too?"

"Yes." I swallow a lump in my throat. "I hope she's everything you wanted."

Jonathan stares down at me, searching my gaze. "I already know she is."

I roll my eyes. "You're so cocky. Some of us, however, who are also meeting our anonymous online pen pals, are quaking in our snow boots."

"Your Mr. Reddit *better* be quaking in his boots. He's got a lot to prove before he's worthy of you."

A blush heats my cheeks. "I'm talking about what he thinks of *me*. I'm nervous. But I'm thinking I'll go baptism by fire and show up in my ugliest Christmas sweater. It plays music. If he can handle that, we can make it through anything."

Jonathan's face breaks into a smile so devastating, it knocks the air out of my lungs. It transforms him, two gorgeous dimples carving down his cheeks, his eyes crinkled handsomely at the corners. His throat works as he laughs loud and deep. Then he drags me into his arms again, hugging me hard as he whispers something into my hair.

"Hey!" I squeak. "Stop smothering me! You finally smiled, and I'm missing it!"

He pulls back and exhales roughly, the smile gone, replaced by something raw and fierce.

"What is it?" I ask.

But he doesn't answer me. He opens my building's door and nudges me inside. And then he sets his gloved hand on the glass of the door. I set my hand there, too.

A moment later, he steps back, turns, and disappears into the snowy night.

"What a strange, lovely man."

My vision's watery, a solitary tear slipping down my cheek, but I smile to myself the whole way up the stairs.

# CHAPTER 13

## PLAYLIST: "YOU AND ME AT CHRISTMAS," WHY DON'T WE

Maybe it's cumulative exhaustion, but for the first time in weeks, my sleep is a black blanket, heavy and dreamless. I wake up rested on Christmas Eve morning and whip up brunch with Eli and June before heading to my parents' to celebrate. It's laughter and good food and music, happy chaos that I love but also requires lots of headphone time.

I sleep dreamlessly that night, too, and wake up to a picture-perfect white Christmas.

Bing sings the famous apropos song as snow drifts from the sky and my parents and I open presents in front of the tree. When the next song starts, my heart twists.

*Little Jack Frost, get lost, get lost.*

I try very hard to banish Jonathan from my thoughts, because tomorrow I meet Mr. Reddit. But after another long day of celebrating, after I tumble into my bed that night, savoring the cozy comfort of my apartment and my cuddly Gingerbread, I'm not as lucky as I have been the past two nights.

This time, my dreams are different. The hands and body

holding me close, loving me, filling me, are gentler, careful, like it's our first time and there's a world to discover between us. It's not Jonathan...and yet something deep in my mind says it is. As I swim to the surface of my dreams, they morph to Jonathan and I saying goodbye outside my apartment, just like after the big sale. Jonathan's staring down at me, something fierce and hot in his gaze as he tells me what he told me that night:

*"Your Mr. Reddit better be quaking in his boots. He's got a lot to prove before he's worthy of you."*

Mr. Reddit... It snags my brain, hooks my thoughts, and yanks me closer, closer to the surface of wakefulness.

Mr. Reddit...

I never told him that name. I only told Mr. Reddit himself.

I'm thrashing among waves where memory and dreams crash and swell, reaching for him, choked and wordless.

*Don't leave! I want to tell him. Don't leave when I've just found you!*

I'm so scared he'll dissolve into midnight-water darkness like he did when we said goodbye. But instead, Jonathan clutches me tight and rips me to the surface, wrapping me in his arms, his mouth taking mine, filling me with words and air and hope. *It's me,* he whispers. *It's always been me.*

Jackknifing up in bed, I gasp. My heart is pounding.

I can't believe it. And yet it's the only thing I can believe.

It's hard to grasp that something so unlikely could be true, but I *know* I've never used the name "Mr. Reddit" around Jonathan. It has to be him. There's no other explanation.

As I rush around, replaying our conversation the night we closed up Bailey's, the questions he asked, his hesitation and tenderness, the wariness in his expression, I become more and more sure. It's him. Jonathan is my Mr. Reddit.

Frantically tugging on fleece-lined leggings, my most

garish fuzzy candy-cane-stripe socks, I falter when I realize my ugly Christmas sweater is nowhere to be seen.

It takes me a moment to recall when I last saw it, and that's when I remember—I left it at Bailey's. My sensory comforts fluctuate from day to day, so I always bring back-up clothes in case what I'm wearing starts to bother me. That last day of work, I brought the heinous sweater and another pair of fleece lined leggings similar to what I'm wearing now, and then failed to bring them home.

I could wear something else. But then I remember Jonathan's breathtaking smile, that deep, rich laugh when I promised to wear the ugly Christmas sweater.

My heart leaps, toe loop after toe loop, as I drag on a cotton long-sleeved tee that I'll wear under the sweater, as I brush my teeth and sort out my wild hair, then run out of the house. A thousand questions storm my mind. How long has he known? When did he figure it out? And why didn't he tell me?

I run, desperate for answers and desperate to see him, slipping on snow, darting around bundled-up slowpokes, my headphones quieting the world to a peaceful hush as snow kisses my skin like a blessing and a promise.

His voice echoes in my head, what he said when I told him I hoped his online friend was everything he wanted.

*I already know she is.*

My heart's flying, I have wings. I soar across the last block leading up to Bailey's, then let myself into the shop. It's quiet inside, a hush of emptiness that I love, compounded by my headphones. Daylight streams in, no lights on. The smell of books and wood polish tickles my nose.

Quickly, I stroll to the back and spot the canvas bag hanging from my clothes hook. I lift it open, yank out my ugly Christmas sweater, then tug it on, which knocks my headphones off and sends a rush of sound into my ears.

"Why haven't you told her?" Mrs. Bailey's voice carries from the bookkeeping room.

I freeze. My breathing sounds a thousand times louder than it should.

"You know why." My stomach drops. That's Jonathan. "She's going to despise me for it."

Blood roars in my ears. I try to breathe, try to make sense of what he's saying.

"Perhaps at first," Mrs. Bailey says quietly. "But once she sees that this is the only way to save the bookshop, she'll understand."

It feels like the floor is crumbling beneath me. I grapple for something to steady myself as I picture it: Mrs. Bailey gently calling me into her office when we come back after the new year, holding my hand, thanking me for all I've given the place, telling me she's sorry, but she has to think of the business first and what Jonathan's brought to it.

Jonathan's words cut to the heart of me: *She's going to despise me for it.*

Desperate to escape, I wend my way through the store as quietly as possible, then slip outside. And then I start to run, streaking down the sidewalk, slipping on ice and snow, tears blurring my vision—

The shriek of a car's horn stops me just in time before I run farther into the crosswalk.

That's when I realize I left my noise-cancelling headphones at the store.

Stumbling back onto the sidewalk, I slump against the coffee shop storefront of all places, where I bought my peppermint hot cocoa six days a week this December, not far from where Trey accosted me and Jonathan came running and everything changed. I gasp for air and stare up at the sky, tiny snowflakes drifting down.

"What do I do?" I whisper. Shutting my eyes, I let the cool wind kiss my skin. I let my heart slow and steady.

And then, like the smooth beauty of fresh-fallen snow, my mind becomes clear. I'm being...ridiculous. I walked into the middle of a conversation between two people who've shown me time and again that they're worthy of my trust and they wouldn't betray me. What am I thinking, running off like this? I'm safe with the Baileys and with Jonathan. There has to be a reason. An explanation—

"Gabby!" Jonathan's voice carries from down the block.

And just like that morning he came running my way, he's running again, hurdling snowbanks and dodging meandering couples. I watch him, tearing toward me, the wind whipping his dark hair, fire burning in those wintergreen eyes.

And then he comes to a halt at my feet, staring at me intensely, my headphones in hand. "I saw them," he says. "And I knew you'd been there, and I don't know what all you heard Gabby, but I promise I'm on your side—"

"I know." I step close, wrapping my hand around his. "I know you are."

His eyes search mine. "You do?"

I smile faintly, taking my headphones, setting them around my neck. "I do. And I'm on your side, too. I don't know what you were discussing. I just know you're afraid to tell me."

"I..." He wraps his hands around my shoulders. "I tried so many times, but I was so scared you'd hate it."

"I heard that part. But I trust you, Jonathan."

"You do?"

"I do."

He frowns. "That's it?"

I nod, blinking away tears. "Yeah. I mean, I wouldn't mind hearing more about whatever ruthless capitalist measures you took to save the place that you're so sure I'm going to despise you for, but I do trust you."

His jaw ticks, like he's steeling himself. "It's...an online version of the bookstore. Hard copies, audio, e-books. Romance readers are our key segment, our number-one target customer. It's going to drive traffic to the website and not necessarily to the brick-and-mortar store, and I know you hate that. I know you want the place brimming with people, like it once was, Gabby, but it was this kind of book-store or no bookstore at all." His eyes search mine. "I wanted it to be safe for you, to keep Bailey's open for you for years and years. I know it's not ideal, but it's the only way—"

"Jonathan," I whisper.

He stares down at me, breathless, wide-eyed. He looks a little terrified.

"Thank you," I tell him, bringing a hand to his face, softly stroking his cheek with my mittened thumb. "For explaining that. For...everything you did. I can't begin to say how much it means, and I want to hear so much more, but the thing is..."

I stare up at Jonathan, and that tear within my heart stitches itself together, as everything I've come to admire and adore in these two men—my nemesis and my friend, my gritty reality and my sweetest escape—fuses into one breath-taking, perfectly imperfect reality.

Him.

"I actually have a date," I whisper, still stroking his cheek. "And I wouldn't want to keep him waiting."

He stares at me very carefully, searching my expression. "As it happens, I do, too."

Tears hover in my eyes, threatening to spill over. "Tell me where."

He steps closer. "The Winter Wonderland at the conservatory," he says softly, "10:00 a.m. sharp. I get to meet the MargaretCATwood of my dreams. And I can only hope—"

I throw myself at him, crush my mouth to his, hot and hard and frantic. His deep, rough groan makes my toes curl, makes sparks dance across my skin. Jonathan's mouth opens for me, his tongue finds mine, and it's hunger and waiting and longing and relief. It's feverish and fervent, panting gasps as we clutch each other like the world's ending and we're holding on for dear life.

"Gabriella." His hands drift down my back, grip my hips, holding me against him.

"Jonathan," I whisper through tears, clutching him tight. "It's you."

He nods, his hands sliding along my back. "You're not disappointed?"

"Disappointed?" I laugh through tears and kiss the corner of his mouth, his jaw, then suck the hollow of his throat, making his hips lurch against mine. "Am I acting disappointed?"

"No," he says roughly, slipping a hand deep inside my hair, massaging my scalp, his other hand drifting up my waist. He kisses me again, deep and velvet hot. "No, you aren't."

"I'm *relieved*." My hands find his back pockets and squeeze his round, hard ass through the fabric. "Thrilled. Beyond happy. My heart was breaking. I wanted both of you, and now I don't have to choose, because it's all...you."

He smiles against our kiss. "Even with my capitalist wiles and the online bookstore?"

I nod and bury my face in his neck, breathing in woodsmoke and wintry forests. "*Especially* with your capitalist wiles and the online bookstore. You saved Bailey's."

"For you."

"For me."

I feel his smile deepen as he nuzzles me, then kisses my

neck down to my collarbone. "I won't work there," he says, "if you don't want. You can have it all for yourself—"

"What?" It's a bucket of ice water right over me. Yanking my hands from his pockets, I pick up my head. Our noses brush, but there's no kiss, only frowning. "I just found you, and now you're leaving me?"

Jonathan's smile is sweet and gentle as he tugs me back into his arms and returns my hands to his back pockets. "You always had me, Gabriella. And I'd love to stay, but not if it won't make you happy."

I melt inside his arms, as Jonathan's hands drift in soothing circles down my waist, then palm my butt affectionately. "It would make me endlessly happy," I tell him. "We're the perfect team, you and I." Our eyes search each other's. I slip a hand from his pocket and brush a dark lock of hair from his face. "When did *you* know?" I ask.

He leans into my touch, his eyes slipping shut. "Our fight after meeting with the Baileys. When I picked up the romance novel, and you made that dig about Jane Austen. It was nearly verbatim what I'd said, what we'd talked about in our chat. I thought I was losing it for a second, imagining things, but then I asked you to name more of your favorite romances, and the ones you pointed out were every single title MCAT had told me. Then I went home and I tried to talk with you on Telegram about work to see if I could get any more clues. When you said you had one coworker who made you miserable and hated the holidays—I *knew* it was you. At least, I was as sure as I could be."

"That's why you said it," I whisper. "When we kissed. *I shouldn't do this. Not yet.*"

Sighing, he opens his eyes. "I wanted to wait until we both knew, until everything was out in the open. Only you were just so perfect, standing there catching snowflakes on your tongue, a smile lighting you up, and I knew you wanted me, even though you were torn. I'd spent thirty minutes with you in my car, listening to the smoke in your voice, watching you squirm your little ass on the seat, rubbing your thighs, staring at my mouth and—God, Gabby, I couldn't stop myself. Not when you were right there with me."

"And when we kissed?" I bite my lip, remembering every hot, wet slick of our tongues and mouths, the way his hands sank into my coat and pinned our hips together.

He's quiet for a moment as he stares at me, holding me tight, so tight, as if he's afraid the moment he lets go, I might vanish. "That's when I prayed, because kissing you was water in a desert, sunlight breaking the horizon, and I was gone for you, no turning back. I'm not a praying man, Gabriella, but I prayed so fucking hard that this wasn't some horrible joke, that you'd be happy when you realized it was me, that whatever cosmic force gave me the gift of stumbling into your life wasn't cruel enough to keep me from always belonging to it."

"Jonathan." I pull away, clasping his face. "My Mr. Reddit. My own grumpy Scrooge McGrinch. It was you. It had to be."

"How did *you* know?" he asks quietly.

I smile so hard my face hurts. "You slipped. The night we closed up, you mentioned Mr. Reddit."

His eyes widen. "Shit. Did I?"

I nod. "I didn't process it until last night—well, early this morning. In my dreams."

His smile is slow and lazy and so arrogantly sensual, I want to kiss it right off his face. "Been dreaming about me, have you, Di Natale?"

I shove him playfully. "I already admitted that the night we closed up." Our humor dies away as I search his eyes. "Why didn't you tell me as soon as *you* suspected it?"

He drifts his knuckle down my cheek, brow furrowed. So serious. "At first, because I was reeling. I needed time to sort it out in my head. And because you hated me, Gabriella.

Especially once I realized how badly I wanted it to work, I realized you needed time to see my less terrible qualities..." He blows out a slow stream of air. "And I needed time to finish the online bookstore build-out, then find the guts to tell you about it. It didn't feel right, the idea of revealing who I was—who *we* were—before I told you everything, including the store."

"I'm so glad it was you," I whisper, throwing my arms around his neck and holding him tight. "I wanted it so badly to be you."

He drinks me in, and a tender smile lifts his mouth. "Look at you."

I peer down at my ugly Christmas sweater with its obnoxious twinkling lights, just waiting for me to flip the hidden switch that'll make it sing. "Brutal, right?"

"Beautiful," he whispers, hands caressing my waist, drawing me close. "The most beautiful. Here." He bends and kisses my temple. "Here." Over my heart. "And here." Then his lips brush mine.

My mouth parts as he wraps me tighter in his arms. This kiss is quiet and gentle, but it doesn't stay that way for long. Before we know it, Jonathan's walking me back until we bump against a wall. I'm starting to tear off his jacket, dragging away mine.

"Wait," he says, even though it sounds like the last thing he wants to say, especially when I slide my hand up his hard thigh, toward where I see clear evidence that he's hurting as badly as I am. "Slow down. Gabriella." God, that voice, deep and commanding, it's just how he sounded in my filthy-aristo-crat, sheet-twisting, hours-of-lovemaking, fantasies. It makes me wild.

"I need you," I tell him.

"God, Gabby." He draws me closer, and his hands slip

down my ass, to my thighs, lifting me up and hiking my legs around his waist. "I need you, too."

"So...about that date?" I tell him. "How about we relocate it? Somewhere with a bed. And no one who needs a damn thing from us. For days."

"My place," he says. "No roommates. No interruptions."

I kiss him hard and deep, then slip slowly down his body. "Your place." I take a step back.

"Hey." He frowns. "Where are you going? We have a date."

"I just need...a quick stop at my place? Fifteen minutes?"

"Fifteen minutes!" he yells like I've told him fifteen years.

"Just to grab a few essentials. Hint: I won't be packing underwear."

His eyes darken. He starts stalking toward me. "I'll drive you. It'll go faster."

A coy smile slips out. "I said fifteen minutes, Frost, and I meant it."

I screech with laughter as he bends and throws me over his shoulder, gently swatting my butt. "Fine. Just be ready to make up for lost time."

"Holy shit." By the sounds of it, June drops her eyeliner pen. "*Scrooge* is Mr. Reddit? Jonathan Frost?"

"It's the stuff of fiction," I tell her, packing the world's most chaotic sleepover bag. My own pillow. Fuzzy socks. Zero underwear. Lots of sweaters. Romance novels. Thin mint cookies. "And yet it's my reality. I'm never going to stop pinching myself."

"You're gonna bang each other's lights out, aren't you?"

"For days." I plop on my bed beside Gingerbread and feed her a handful of treats. "Don't miss me too much," I tell her.

"And don't worry, I'll bring Jonathan by soon so you can meet him."

Gingerbread purrs like an engine missing its muffler, and while it's probably because I gave her three times more treats than normal, I'm choosing to believe that it's her excitement about getting to meet the man waiting not-so-patiently downstairs in his SUV.

"Gabby?" June's voice wafts from the Jack and Jill bathroom connecting our bedrooms.

"Yeah?"

"What are the chances? Have you wrapped your head around that?"

Glancing toward the window facing the street and Jonathan's car below, I picture him—dark hair, stern features, wintergreen eyes, that soft, warm smile only for me.

"Terrifyingly slim," I tell her. "I'm the luckiest person in the world."

Easing off the bed, I throw my bag over my shoulder. It feels like Christmas morning all over again.

June catches me in the mirror, observing my dazed smile, the hearts dancing in my eyes. "Wow," she says. "You're a goner."

I smile even wider. "Yeah."

"Well, he just better deserve you," she mutters, back at her eyeliner.

"Considering he built out an online store with enough projected profits that Bailey's will be safe indefinitely, and he did it all for me—"

"God*dammit*." A streak of kohl black eyeliner marks her temple. June tosses the pen aside and spins to face me, tears in her eyes. "No more of this mushy stuff. It's messing up my cat-eye. Why must you torture me with heartfelt, makeup-wrecking drivel?"

"Because I want your support. Yours and Eli's."

She snorts, dabbing her eyes. "We know Eli's all for it."

"True. He's already planning our double wedding with him and Luke. He's over the moon. I want you to be, too, June."

Crossing the small space between us, she hugs me tight, her voice hoarse as she kisses my temple. "If anyone deserves a happy ending, it's you." She smacks my butt as I run out of the bathroom. "Now go be naughty!"

# CHAPTER 14

PLAYLIST: "UNDER THE CHRISTMAS
LIGHTS," GWEN STEFANI

Heart aglow, I bound down the stairs of my apartment building, burst out of the door, and launch myself into Jonathan's arms.

He laughs, warm and deep, as he kisses my cheeks, my nose, my mouth. "I missed you," he says. "Worst fifteen minutes ever."

"Felt like fifteen days." I smile up at him, taking his hand when he offers it so I can step over another snowbank and into my seat in his SUV.

Jonathan drives, and we bicker. I complain about him observing the speed limits when there's just a little snow on the road and I desperately want to be at his place, already naked. He reminds me that he's very much on board with being at his place and already naked, but *I'm* the one who demanded a pit-stop. Honestly, after behaving ourselves for two weeks, it feels great. It feels like slipping into my softest shirt and under my coziest blanket—familiar and safe and right.

"Satisfied?" he says, throwing the car into park.

"Not yet." Climbing the center console, I straddle his lap

the way I wanted to the first time he drove me home. "But soon I will be."

Jonathan can't even hide his smile as I slip my hands up his shirt, careful of his infusion site above his hip, and tease his stomach and chest. His eyes drift shut as I kiss my way up his throat, his jaw, his cheekbones, then the corner of his mouth. "I nearly ran a red light back there," he mutters, slipping his hands down my hips to my backside, caressing, kneading.. "Thanks to you and your sexual demands."

"You like my sexual demands."

"I do," he admits, moving me against him where he's hard and straining against his slacks. "But I'd like them better upstairs on the bed in front of the fire."

I wrench myself away, tumbling like a lopsided snowball back onto my seat and throwing open the door. "Hurry up!"

Laughing, Jonathan runs around the car and sweeps me into his arms. I wrap myself around him like an oversized koala as he unlocks his building's door and jogs up the stairs. "Impressive fitness," I tell him.

"Hockey's good for something."

"Running up a flight of stairs with your sexually demanding woman and not being breathless?"

He arches an eyebrow as he opens the door to his place. "Yes, but more generally—" He kicks the door shut behind us. "Stamina."

With the push of a remote button, flames dance to life in his apartment's living room fireplace.

"Wow," I whisper.

He grins and says, "Hold that thought."

In an impressive display of strength, Jonathan drags his low platform bed from its corner in the studio space, across the room, until it rests, covered in cozy blankets right in front of the fire.

Before I can say a word, Jonathan slips my coat off of my

shoulders, then hangs it up. Pressing a featherlight kiss to my neck, he breathes me in. I sigh, letting my head fall back on his shoulder, how I've wanted to. His arms wrap around me from behind as I reach back and palm him over the hard, thick outline of his erection.

"I want you so bad, I can barely see straight," he says roughly.

"That festive firecracker at work got you horny?" I whisper. "With her generous hips and bedhead curls and a penchant for pushing your buttons?"

He groans a laugh. "It's like you speak from experience or something. Got a colleague you've been hot for?"

"You drive me wild." I spin in his arms and growl the words against his mouth as we kiss, biting his lip. "You are designed to make me feral."

He clasps my face and kisses me again, hard and hungry, walking us toward the bed. "You have no idea."

"I want to know."

"From the moment I realized the statistical likelihood that MCAT was you," he says between kisses, "given all the overlapping circumstances and evidence, I've been *gone*. All I'd been repressing around you, Gabriella"—*kiss*—"all I'd denied myself from imagining with MCAT"—*kiss*—"coalesced. I've been wrecked. I had to watch you walk around the store and glare at me, still hating my guts. And then I had to go home and beat off in the shower every night because you made me furious and so fucking hard."

My mouth falls open. "I want a replay later."

"I'm so glad it's you, Gabriella." He's past the horny talk, on to the romance, tugging me against him, teasing my nipples over my sweater. "I wouldn't have been able to stand it any other way."

"Jonathan," I whisper, deliriously happy with how he's touching me. "Me, too."

Taking my hand, he sits on the bed and tugs me down, the fire dancing behind us.

I tumble onto his lap, staring down at Jonathan as he smooths errant curls away from my face and tucks one behind my ear. I slip my hand beneath his shirt, up his chest to rest over his heart, and then I kiss him. Our tongues touch, and it's flint and steel, air rushing out of us, both of us toeing off our shoes, crawling back on the bed, attacking each other's clothes.

"You smell incredible," I whisper, burying my nose in his neck, breathing him in. "How do you smell so incredible?"

He huffs a laugh, but it turns tight and ragged as I lick his Adam's apple, tasting his skin. "It's just my bodywash. When I realized harsh scents gave you headaches, I stopped wearing cologne and switched to this instead."

I sigh with pleasure, shamelessly rubbing myself against him, touching him, tasting him. "That's unacceptably sweet."

"I tried," he admits, kissing a wildly sensitive spot on my neck, nipping my ear with his teeth. "In very stealthy ways."

"Clothes," I whine. "Off. All of them."

He clasps the hem of my shirt and starts to lift. "Tell me, Gabriella. What you want. What you don't. Promise."

"I promise," I tell him, kissing his jaw, palming him over his pants where he's hard and tenting the fabric.

Jonathan peels away my sweater, then my shirt beneath, baring my breasts to him since I'm not wearing a bra. What was the point when he was just going to take it off anyway?

His hands shake as he glides them up my waist and gently cups my breasts. His thumbs circle my nipples as he kisses my neck, my jaw, my mouth. "How are you so beautiful?"

"Because I'm yours."

"Mine," he whispers, bending to kiss my breasts, dragging each nipple in his mouth with long slow sucks that send bolts of pleasure down my stomach, lower, where I'm wet and dying for his touch.

Pressing me back onto the bed, he tugs down my leggings. And when he sees me, he sucks in a ragged breath. His hands drift around to my bare backside and tug me closer. "I want to drive you wild," he mutters.

I sit up on elbows, so I can see him better, watch his hands traveling my body. "Please do. You've been much too nice the past two weeks. I'm in withdrawal."

Laughing, he presses a kiss to my hip, then my stomach. On the first, gentle kiss to my clit, I buckle and fall back on the bed.

He grins, looking supremely pleased. "That impressive, eh?"

I push myself back up. "Just slow down there, Mr. Frost. I have some undressing to do, myself."

First I slip off his sweater, deepest jade, like evergreens at midnight. Then I peel off his tight, white undershirt, baring a beautiful, muscled body dusted in dark hair. I touch his hard chest and flat, dusky nipples. Then I kiss and suck them, making him groan.

When I get to his slacks, I stop myself. My hand rests at his hip, near his infusion site and the pocket where I see his pump. "Show me?"

"I—" He clears his throat. "I like to unplug, so I can move around freely and not worry about tugging on the tubing." I watch him carefully as he disconnects the thin clear tube attached to his pump from the small disc adhered to his skin, then gathers it in his hand. "Just don't let me fall asleep after you wear me out." He flashes me a grin. "It's best to plug back in afterward."

"I won't let you fall asleep," I tell him quietly, softly tracing the *V* along his hip, up the strong muscles knit to his ribs.

Extracting the pump from his pocket, Jonathan sets both pump and tubing safely on the nearby coffee table. And when he turns back, I give him a long, slow kiss.

"What was that for?" he says.

"Because I wanted to."

He smiles, recognizing his own words from the night he drove me home, the night everything started to change. "I wanted to do much more than help you into my car, Gabriella."

"That feeling was mutual," I tell him, pushing Jonathan onto his back. I lower his zipper, then drag his pants and boxer briefs down. God, he's beautiful, all long, powerful muscles and a thick, jutting erection. I kiss his big, muscly thighs, his lean hips, every inch of him that's hard beneath firm, warm skin.

"Gabriella," he whispers, yanking me close, kissing my neck, my collarbone, gently tugging one of my nipples with his mouth, then the other. "I want you to come."

"I want us both to." I smile as he pushes me onto my back and crawls down my body.

"You first," he says, all growl and command that makes me spread my legs shamelessly wide. "Like this, huh?" he asks coyly, kissing his way up my thighs.

"God, yes. And I got tested recently. No STIs."

"Same. On both counts," he says softly. A pained groan leaves him as he strokes me with his fingertips. "Fuck, you're wet. And soft. And gorgeous." Then he drops down and drags me by the hips until I'm right in his face, and his tongue is exactly where I want it.

He starts soft rhythmic laps of my clit, then slips one finger deep inside, working me steadily, watching me, learning what makes me melt and moan.

It's not fast for me, but Jonathan doesn't seem to mind one bit. He licks and tastes and teases, strokes me with his fingers. He says every filthy thing I knew he would and a few I didn't see coming, words that make my back arch, makes desire sing through my veins.

I'm hot and yet I'm shivering, pleasure swirling deep inside me, radiating out to my breasts and throat, my fingertips and toes. "Feels so good," I whisper.

A deep, satisfied hum rumbles in his throat. "Good."

"*So* good," I tell him again, when he finds that perfect rhythm of his mouth and hands, his tongue swirling my clit, two fingers rubbing my G-spot. I arch off the bed. "Don't stop. Just like that. Please don't stop."

Jonathan groans again, so clearly turned on by turning *me* on. He thrusts his pelvis into the mattress in rhythm with his fingers' movement, his eyes shut like he's in ecstasy. I want to watch him fucking the bed because he's so desperate for me, but as he works me harder, faster, my eyes fall shut and pleasure spools, tight and white hot through my limbs. I bend my legs, locking them around his shoulders. Canting my hips against his mouth, I slip my fingers into his hair. "Oh God, I'm so close. Please, I'm so—"

I shatter, gasping again and again as he chases my tremoring hips with his tongue, stretching out my orgasm until I gently push him away, begging for no more.

"Gabriella," he says, leaning over me.

"Jonathan," I tell him breathlessly, drawing his hips close to mine. "No STIs. We covered that. I take the pill every morning."

His thick length, dark and wet at the tip rubs against me. "No condoms?" he grits out.

"I don't like the feel of them. I understand their importance, and I can use them if needed, but if you're okay with not—"

"I'm very okay with not." He cups my breast and moves

against me, working me up to another orgasm with sure, slow strokes of his cock over my clit.

I'm so close, rubbing against him, begging nonsensically, until I finally manage to say, "Inside me. I want you inside me."

Jonathan kisses me hungrily and starts to ease himself in, but it's tight and I start to panic. His hand slips into my hair, massaging my scalp. He kisses my cheek, my nose, my cupid's bow. "Relax for me, Gabriella."

I moan at the command in his voice, feeling my body loosen responsively. Gently, he rocks in a little deeper.

"Breathe, beautiful," he says against my ear, before pressing a long, hot kiss to my neck. He's big, and it's tight, but I'm wet, so wet, and he kisses me, praises me, until I feel him seated fully inside.

I grip his shoulders, arching up into him. "I need you."

"I'm here." He groans as he pumps into me, his grip hard and possessive on my hip. "I'm right here, and you are goddamn exquisite. Fuck, you feel so good. So tight and warm."

Jonathan holds me close, stroking a place deep inside me that makes my breath catch, makes my hips buck into his frantically.

He wraps his arms tighter around me, his weight pushing me into the mattress, making me feel every nudge of his hips, the steady rub of his pelvis against my clit. He kisses my neck, my mouth, my breasts. It's fast and desperate, and I start to shake beneath him, to buck and cry, and then I'm coming in such powerful waves, only his body can hold me down.

"Gabby," he whispers. "Oh, God, I feel you."

He pulls back and strokes into me, faster, harder, air rushing out of him. "I'm gonna come, Gabby."

I hold him close as he drops down again and slips his arms

around me, between my back and the bed. He drives into me, sending me higher up the mattress with each deep, pained grunt. I feel him let go, feel him surrender his body to mine as I hold him tight.

"Oh God, Gabby. Oh fuck—"

"I want it all," I tell him through a hard kiss, sinking my hands into his ass, urging him on. "Give me everything."

On a shout, he thrusts into me and spills, long and hot, frantic punches of his hips as he calls my name, until he's spent. After a quiet moment and a dozen tender, breathless kisses, Jonathan eases off my body and tugs me into his arms. Content and dazed, we search each other's eyes.

"Wow," I whisper.

"'Wow' is right," he says on a soft smile, his hand wrapping around my waist. He stares at me so intently, that soft smile deepening.

"What is it?"

He sighs happily. "You're here."

Now my smile mirrors his. "I'm here. We just had amazing sex. What did I do to deserve that? Have I been naughty? Or nice?"

He laughs deep and rich, drawing me closer in his arms, kissing me slowly. "Both."

Pulling back, I slide my hands through his hair and examine him. "Do you know how lucky we are? That we found each other not once but twice?"

He searches my eyes, his expression serious. "The luckiest."

"Why do you look like that makes you sad?"

He tugs me closer and kisses me again. "I'm too familiar with probability and statistics."

"What does that mean?"

"It means one wrong move," he says quietly, his forehead against mine, "one single misstep, and I'd have missed you.

And I don't want that world. I never want a world without you."

"Jonathan." I cup his face, searching his eyes. They're wet. "Hey. It's all right. I'm here."

He crushes me in his arms and buries his face in my neck, breathing me in. "Sugar plums," he whispers. "You smell like tart plums and cinnamon sugar, and it's the best fucking smell in the world."

I smile, sliding my fingers through his hair in a way that I hope soothes him. "You've been a little stressed, haven't you? You've had all this knowledge and worry bottled up beneath that tough-guy surface."

He nuzzles me and hides in the crook of my neck, kissing me there softly. "That last night at work, when you told me where you were meeting him—me—I wanted to tell you so badly. And so many times in those three days we were apart, I almost texted you, almost called, almost went on Telegram and told you everything, but..." He pulls away, holding my eyes. "but I just couldn't do it. I kept freaking out, that I'd tell you and you'd truly despise me for what I'd done with the store, and then I'd lose you—"

"Never," I tell him.

"I know that now," he says quietly, almost to himself, playing with a lock of my hair. "That's why I met Mrs. Bailey, for advice about how to finally get the courage to tell you."

"You figured it out." I smile at him. "We both did."

"Yeah." His eyes search mine. "We did."

And for a long time, we lie there in the quiet, nothing but the soft dance of the fire's flames, the sound of our breath and whispered voices as we touch and stare at each other, bursts of laughter and smiles, piecing together the past year, stitching every part of ourselves and our past into one glorious, promising whole.

After a sweet, slow kiss, Jonathan nods his chin toward

the miniature Christmas tree nestled on the mantle of his fireplace, sparkling with tiny twinkly lights. "This is what you did to me," he grumbles. "I have a Christmas tree. I'm an agnostic who, despite my business acumen, loathes the empty consumerist impulses of the season, and here I am, with a Christmas tree on my mantle."

"I don't think it's tiny enough. And it's definitely missing a fingernail-sized tree topper." I kiss him softly. "It's the sweetest thing, Jonathan, but just so you know...you don't have to love the holidays. I love them enough for both of us."

It's quiet for a minute. He traces my breasts with a fingertip, turning my nipples hard and tender. "It's not so much that I *hate* the holidays," he says. "I just don't...have many happy memories from them. My parents weren't good together. They always fought badly, but they were at their worst around the holidays—screaming fights, slamming doors, driving off at night and not coming back until the next day.

"My sister Liz, who you met, she's older, and she bore such a burden around that time of year, trying to offset my parents' animosity, to make things extra 'festive' and 'happy' for me. As I got older, that just struck me as deeply unfair and oppressive, this pressure and guilt if we weren't always 'cheerful' simply because it was the month of December and 'Christmas was coming!'"

I peer up at him, gliding my fingers through his hair. "I'm sorry. That makes complete sense."

He turns his head and kisses my palm. "You don't need to be sorry, Gabriella. And all that to say, while I don't have many positive associations with the holidays..." He gently cups my breast, then kisses me slowly. "I think, going forward I will."

I sigh into our kiss, but then I pull away, meeting his eyes. "I'm still sorry it was hard. For you and Liz."

"Thank you, Gabby." He's kissing me more, trying to move past the moment. And I understand. But I need him to know this. Sitting up, I press Jonathan onto his back, then straddle his lap. I set my hands on his shoulders and peer down, one eyebrow arched.

He gives me an amused, affectionate smile. "I see what you're doing. And you're not *quite* there." Gently, with his index finger, he lifts the arch of my eyebrow higher. "Better."

"Good. Now listen up, champ."

"Champ, huh?"

"You heard me." I drop the act and settle my weight on him, making Jonathan exhale roughly and grip my waist. "Especially now that I know why the holidays aren't your favorite, I need you to believe me—that, yes, I love holiday cheer and festive fun, but not as much as I love..." I search his eyes, afraid to say something so true so soon. Instead, I tell him, "I don't want you to change for me. I want you, just as you are, Jonathan Frost. That's more than enough."

His eyes search mine. "I believe you. And I know you'd never expect me to change. I just think it'll be pretty damn impossible not to love the holidays just a *little*, now that I get to share them with you."

I bite my lip so I won't cry. "That's...absurdly sweet, Jonathan."

Smiling, he drags me down and wraps me in his arms.

"Gabriella," he says quietly, hiking my leg around his waist.

He's hard again, snug and hot between my thighs. "Jonathan," I whisper.

His lips brush mine as he tells me, "Gabriella, I love you. I don't expect you to say it back, but I can't go a moment longer without you knowing the truth."

*I gasp, joyful and thrilled, but he kisses me before I can say a word, a bone-melting, world-tipping kiss. "'I cannot fix on the hour,'" he says quietly, "'or the spot, or the look or the words, which laid the foundation. It is too long ago. I was in the middle before I knew that I had begun.'"*

Warmth spills from my heart into my hands, touching him, into my lips, kissing him. My love is a glowing sunrise pouring over hard, snowy ground. "*Pride and Prejudice,*" I whisper.

He nods. "Austen's best."

"Yeah, it really is."

"There's a lot more to the romance genre, I'll have you know, but *P and P* is some good shit. So much frustration," he growls against my skin, "and longing and *work*—"

"Before they're ready to set aside their judgment and preconceived notions." I search his eyes. "To be brave and lay down their defenses. That's when they see each other clearly. And they fall madly in love."

He kisses me, deep and slow. I taste how much he wants me. "And they earn their happy ending."

"No more unrequited longing," I tell him.

"No more being brave on your own," he says. "Now we're brave together."

"Together." I smile up at him and hold his eyes. "I love you, too, you know."

He grins, twirling a ribbon of my hair around his finger, then bringing it to his lips for a reverent kiss. "I know."

I study him, stern features softened as he meets my gaze and flashes an even brighter smile. I've mussed his dark, lovely hair. There's a flush on his cheeks. His pale green eyes sparkle. I want a hundred lifetimes to look at that face and love him.

"I love you," I whisper, reaching between us, stroking him as he rocks against me. "And I want you. This way. A thousand ways."

"God, yes," he groans. He eases inside me, as we lay on

our sides, facing each other, one hand low on my back, the other between us, rubbing my clit. I cling to him, riding his length, staring into his eyes, bathed in firelight and tangled sheets and the heat of his body against mine.

It's not frantic this time, but deliciously slow and patient, drawn out so long because we're desperate for it not to end. Jonathan's hips roll with mine, his grip tightens. And when his thumb circles my clit *just* right, I start to come around him.

Holding my eyes, Jonathan clutches me tight and buries himself in me as he finds his own release. And afterward, we lay tangled in each other's arms, breathless, bathed in firelight and the tiniest Christmas tree's twinkling lights.

My hand over his pounding heart, his hand over mine, I kiss the man I love. My happiest happy ending.

He kisses me, too, soft and cool as falling snow, and whispers what I already know, down to my bones—

I'm his happy ending, too.

# EPILOGUE — JONATHAN

## PLAYLIST: "MERRY CHRISTMAS, MARRY ME," CROFTS FAMILY

She leans out of the doorway, winter wind caressing her honey-brown curls, whipping her red sweater dress against her lush body. I was never much for presents, but I now have even less use for them—Gabriella is gift enough.

"Merry Christmas!" shouts her latest customer from down the sidewalk, a kid bundled up and wearing fuzzy white earmuffs that evoke old, sweet memories and a pang of nostalgia.

"Merry Christmas!" Gabriella calls back, waving and smiling brightly.

And just like always, her radiant joy hits me like an arrow to the heart.

And just like always, she stands outside too long in nothing but a flimsy dress to keep her warm.

"Mrs. Frost."

She glances over shoulder, curls swinging, sparkling hazel eyes, and deep, sweet dimples in her cheeks. God, she's beautiful. "Yes, Mr. Frost?"

"I'd like my wife and I to ring in the new year tonight *without* a case of hypothermia on our hands—"

"Oh, good grief. I got a little shivery on that solstice hike. I was not *hypothermic*."

"Not what June said."

She rolls her eyes, turning back and waving once more to the kid outside. "You and June are two overprotective peas in a pod."

"Also known as pragmatists who love you despite your impractical attachment to wading through hip-high snow." Stepping behind her, I wrap my arms around her waist. "How about you join me in the heat?"

Sighing, Gabby lets me spin her around and tug her inside, then shut the door behind us. And don't you know, she's shivering. Slipping her arms around my waist, she burrows against my chest for warmth.

"Freezing your ass off for customers," I mutter.

"Seeing off a patron makes them feel appreciated and special," she tells me primly. "It's this thing called a positive customer service experience, which our market research indicates is a leading reason customers report returning to the brick-and-mortar store. Someone around here has to make it happen, seeing as the other guy who hangs around the place is a real grinch."

"Mm." I run my hands along her arms, warming her up. "You oughta give him the boot."

Her smile's back in full, breathtaking force. "I think I'll keep him. He might look like he's doing more harm than good, scowling at patrons while they thumb through his books—"

"*Our* books. And this isn't a library. They browse it, they buy it."

"Our books," she concedes, her fingers slipping through my

hair. "This guy, though, he's deceptive. At first I thought, 'He's such a Scrooge!' Turns out, he's got a heart of gold. He invested well and made this bookstore solidly profitable over the past ten years, then guess what he did? He started *donating* money!"

I *boo-hiss* because I know it'll make her laugh.

"Even worse," she says around fits of laughter, "he had the gall to co-found a charity with me dedicated to—wait for it." She leans in conspiratorially. "Wintertime needs. People who could use help paying to heat and light their homes. Coats, boots, hats, and gloves for those without them. *And* a massive fund to buy gifts for kids whose families can't afford them."

"Sounds like a real piece of work."

"Oh, he is." She wraps her arms around my neck and sways us side to side. "But I love him. So very, very much."

My hands slide down her waist, and I walk her back until she's pressed against the door. "Jonathan!" she hisses. "What are you doing? We're going to traumatize some poor kid who just wants to come in and buy a book—"

"Store's closed." I flip over the sign, lock the bolt, then sweep her into my arms, carrying Gabby toward the newest feature of the store: a sturdy wooden ladder that glides across the built-in bookshelves. It fulfilled Gabriella's fantasy of recreating Belle's moment in *Beauty and the Beast*, and it fulfilled my fantasy of lounging by the fire and seeing right up her dress.

"We can't just close the store," she says. "We have a bottom line to maintain, Mr. Frost. Crucial profits will be lost."

"God, I love when you talk money to me. Thankfully, after having a long, hard—" I set her on a rung of the ladder, slide her dress up her thighs to those decadently full hips, then spread her legs until she can feel and appreciate the double-meaning in my words "—look at the numbers, I've determined we can afford to lose fifteen minutes' worth of business."

"Fifteen minutes?" She arches an eyebrow. "Awfully confident in your seductive powers after all these years, Jonathan Frost."

"Damn right."

Her head falls back against the ladder as I kiss her throat, lower the neckline of her dress, and free her breasts. I tease each nipple with my mouth in hard, rhythmic sucks, while my thumbs trace her silky inner thighs in slow circles that drive her wild.

"What did I do to deserve a mid-morning orgasm?" she asks, a dreamy smile on her gorgeous face.

"You've been naughty, Gabriella."

She bites her lip. "It was just a little holiday prank."

"It was a very real-looking audit from the IRS, until I saw it was addressed to Jonathan Scrooge McGrinch."

She cackles. "Gotta keep you on your toes, Frost."

I nip her neck, then chase it with a wet, hot kiss. "You're lucky I love you."

"So lucky," she breathes, her hands gliding down my back, then lower, pulling me close. "Now remind me just how lucky, please."

"I'm the lucky one," I tell her as she yanks open my buckle, still mindful of my nearby infusion site and tubing at my hip.

Pressing a hot, slow kiss to the hollow of my throat, she slips my pump from my front pocket to the back one, like a sexy pickpocket, so it's out of the way, then drags down the zipper of my slacks and frees my cock, which throbs, hard and aching for her.

The moment I sink inside her, we both moan with relief.

How many times have I done this? How many places and

ways? And yet every time with her, I'm desperate and undone, aching for the moment I'm inside her.

On the first deep thrust of my hips, her eyes drift shut. She sinks her hands into my shirt and bites her lip. Hard. The sight of it makes me groan rough and low in my throat.

Gabby clenches around me, torturing me because she loves to, and I couldn't live without it. It makes me grip the ladder hard and wrap her tight inside my other arm. "Behave yourself."

She laughs breathily. "I'd rather not."

Another clench around me makes me buck into her. "Fuck, Gabby."

Watching her full lips part in pleasure, those feline hazel eyes flutter open and find mine, I touch her clit just how she loves, in tight, fast circles that make her work herself over every inch of me and ride me hard, chasing her release. The ladder creaks. Gabby's cries grow louder, uninhibited as they echo around us, smoky and breathless. I soak up each desperate call of my name, every gasped *yes* and *please* and *I love you* until she comes, hard and breathless, and takes me with her.

After we've cleaned up and straightened out our clothes, I sweep Gabby into my arms again and carry her to one of the wingback chairs in front of the fire.

"What's with all the carrying?" she says, arms thrown around my neck, head lolling heavily on my shoulder. Her voice is languid and satisfied. I live for that sound in her voice.

"Because one brief carry across an apartment threshold after your wedding is absolutely not enough."

She laughs. "After that performance on the ladder, if I hadn't already done it, I'd marry your fine ass in a heartbeat, Jonathan Frost."

"I know," I tell her, kissing her as I set her down on the

ground. "But it's nice to know you married me years ago and for more than my ruthless capitalist machinations' power to set you up for life with chocolate milk."

"Hot cocoa," she growls playfully, clasping my waist and kissing me again. Her eyes search mine. "Speaking of ruthless capitalist machinations, I'm still not sure I forgive you for what you pulled after the wedding."

"Gabriella." I sit in one of the wingbacks and haul her onto my lap. "What I 'pulled' was a wedding gift."

Toeing off her boots, she curls up close to my chest, nestled right where I want her. With a fingertip she traces my wedding ring—a broad white-gold band etched with snowflakes inside it, an exact replica of the more delicate band adorning her finger.

"Buying us this place is the most unforgivably romantic thing, Mr. Frost. But I'm trying my best to let bygones be bygones." Her expression grows serious as she peers up at me. "It was the best gift ever. And I'll never be able to give you a gift like that in return."

"Gabriella. Love of my life, you already have."

She tips her head, her smile soft and curious. "What gift is that?"

I set her hand over my heart and kiss her with all I've got. "You."

## THE END

# ACKNOWLEDGMENTS

Jonathan and Gabby's story was a joy to write. It was my first time writing a novella, in single point of view, and a holiday romance, and going for it felt sort of like that first time down a "real" hill when you learn to ski—a daunting, exhilarating, accelerating adventure that starts off a little nervously and ends in a *Wow-I've-got-to-do-that-again* thrill. I am beyond delighted by how their story turned out, and I'm so very grateful to those who helped make it possible.

My deepest thanks to Michelle, Jessica, and the entire team at Kobo who supported this project every step of the way; to my irreplaceable editor, Jackie; and last but most certainly not least, to my phenomenal agent, Samantha. A very special thanks also to Ellie and Izzy, whose feedback on this romance's structure, nuances, and representation was invaluable.

Finally, thank you with all my heart to the readers who make this author journey possible. Every thoughtful, kind email and comment, every heartfelt message—I treasure them and you beyond words.

XO,
Chloe

# ABOUT THE AUTHOR

Chloe writes romances reflecting her belief that everyone deserves a love story. Her stories pack a punch of heat, heart, and humor, and often feature characters who are neurodivergent like herself. When not dreaming up her next book, Chloe spends her time wandering in nature, playing soccer, and most happily at home with her family and mischievous cats.

To sign up for Chloe's latest news, new releases, and special offers, please visit her website (www.chloeliese.com) and subscribe!

# BOOKS BY CHLOE LIESE

### **The Bergman Brothers Novels**

Only When It's Us (#1)

Always Only You (#2)

Ever After Always (#3)

With You Forever (#4)

Everything for You (#5)

If Only You (#6)

Only and Forever (#7)

### **Holiday Romance**

The Mistletoe Motive